SANDRA EDEN'S WAR

Mike Low

SilverWood

Published in 2019 by SilverWood Books

SilverWood Books Ltd
14 Small Street, Bristol, BS1 1DE, United Kingdom
www.silverwoodbooks.co.uk

ISBN 978-1-78132-912-2 (paperback)

British Library Cataloguing in Publication Data
A CIP catalogue record for this book is
available from the British Library

Page design and typesetting by SilverWood Books
Printed on responsibly sourced paper

MIKE LOW spent most of his career working for Rolls-Royce PLC, where he was involved in the production of aero engines for the Civil Aerospace and Defence Aerospace divisions. Mike also worked in the manufacture of other Rolls-Royce power plants for use in the Marine and Nuclear divisions.

In 2013 Mike published his first book, *The Bleedin' Obvious Way to Improve Quality in Your Business*, which was based upon his experience of the quality control operations of businesses around the world that were suppliers to Rolls-Royce. His second, *Saviour of the Free World: The Story of the Rolls-Royce Merlin Aero Engine*, followed in 2015. Mike's first novel *The Voyage of An Luchog* was published in 2017.

Mike is married and lives in Somerset. To find out more about Mike, visit his website at: www.mikelow.co.uk.

ALSO BY MIKE LOW

The Bleedin' Obvious Way to Improve Quality in Your Business
Saviour of the Free World: The Story of the Rolls-Royce Merlin Aero Engine
The Voyage of An Luchog

All available from SilverWood Books, Waterstones,
Amazon and other retailers

This book is dedicated to all those brave and valiant members of the SOE. May their contribution and sacrifice never be forgotten.

Acknowledgements

My thanks to my darling wife for proofreading various draft copies and to the brilliant people at SilverWood who helped in so many ways. Any errors or omissions are, of course, entirely my own.

Introduction

This is the story of one woman's involvement in the fight to help free Europe from the oppression of Nazism. Sandra Eden, a British Special Operations Executive (SOE) agent, is parachuted into France just a few weeks before D-Day, 6 June 1944, with the task of helping the French Resistance severely disrupt German troop movements and supply lines in and around the Allied invasion area of Normandy. The story is, of course, fiction, though much of the content is based on research into the actions of various female, and male, SOE agents, who worked in so many extraordinarily courageous and selfless ways to ensure the survival of the continuing freedom that we in the Western world still enjoy today.

The tale is one of incredible bravery and self-sacrifice combined with an insight into the actions of the SOE, the organisation set up by Winston Churchill in 1940 with the direct assignment to 'set Europe ablaze' and help shorten the most bloody war in the history of mankind.

SANDRA EDEN'S WAR

Chapter 1

James turned the Lysander to starboard, and with an easy movement his plane banked around until it was facing where Sandra had just jumped. James wanted to watch Sandra float downwards safely before he tree-hopped back to England. It was still quite dark, though with the moonlight shining he felt sure he would be able to see the whiteness of her parachute as she drifted towards the ground.

Now, where was she? James was struggling to catch sight of anything that looked like an open parachute. She must be somewhere over there, he thought, as he peered intently into the distance. Then he saw it.

'Oh no!' he cried to himself. There, just a few hundred yards away and well below his aircraft, he caught sight of the thin, straggling, useless white parachute, with Sandra attached to its end as it hurtled towards the ground. There was nothing he could do. His mind was racing, and his stomach tied itself in knots. She's going to die – oh no, oh no, NO! Never before had he felt so utterly helpless.

After this dreadful momentary distraction, James brought the Lysander back on course and headed towards the Channel, keeping the plane as low as possible to avoid any anti-aircraft fire or detection by German fighters. He was shocked and dismayed, having just watched the certain death of someone he had met and known for only a few hours, yet had come to think of as someone very special indeed. What a waste of a life!

James tried to concentrate on returning to base safely, yet his mind was in turmoil. He had so enjoyed meeting Sandra shortly before they had taken off from Tangmere to fly over to Normandy. She had struck him as an extraordinary woman, confident and assured, good-looking and with a keen sense of humour. She had bowled him over, and now she would be dead. No one could survive what he had just witnessed, a fall to the ground from 3,000 feet. She would have hit the ground at more than 100 miles per hour. He would have to report all he had seen to the station commander when he returned. What a sad, sad night this had been.

Flight Lieutenant James Silverstone was an experienced RAF pilot. He had flown Hurricane fighters during the Battle of Britain and was shot down over France and taken prisoner by the Nazis in 1942. He had escaped from his prisoner of war camp and managed to get home through Spain with help from the French Resistance. After a period of rest, he had returned to the RAF and spent some months helping SOE agents parachute and land in occupied France. This was the only time he had witnessed a Roman Candle, as a failed parachute-opening was nicknamed. He felt sick at heart.

The flight from Normandy to RAF Tangmere airfield took around one hour, and all the while James tried to shut out what he had just witnessed, but it was impossible. The sight of the failed chute hurtling Sandra towards certain death would be with him forever. James could now see the coast of England, which was no more than a few miles away. He would soon be back at base. The rain that had followed him all the way from Normandy showed no sign of abating. After a short while, he spotted the runway and, with the minimum of trouble, safely landed the Lysander. James continued taxiing until he reached the main hangar, where he parked at the entrance and switched off the engine.

'He's back,' said the air traffic controller through his microphone. He was on a direct line to Major Edward Sheppard – the Air Officer Commanding for the base – who was sitting at his desk, waiting for that news. Major Sheppard would soon be interviewing James.

'Her chute didn't open, sir. She must be dead. It was not a pretty sight.' James spoke quickly and got straight to the point while looking directly at Major Sheppard.

'Didn't open? What on earth is going wrong with our chutes? That's the second failure in a fortnight. I will contact the chute factory and get someone to oversee what the hell they're doing. This is no good!'

The frustration showed by Major Sheppard did little to mitigate the sense of loss felt by James. He wished the Major would show some compassion for Sandra, but that was not forthcoming.

'Will her family be told, sir?' James asked.

'Yes, of course. I will contact the necessary authorities and make sure they're told. That will be all, Silverstone.'

James saluted, turned and left the Major's office.

The Major waited for the door to close and then leaned forward to pick up his phone. He was going to contact SOE headquarters first.

'Linda, get me through to London. Baker Street. As soon as possible.'

'Yes, sir. Right away.'

Linda had been assigned to Major Sheppard as his secretary for the last six months. She did occasionally wish he was a little more polite, but there was a war on, and she thought, well, let's just get on with it. She rang the required number and sat waiting for an answer.

Eventually a female voice said: 'Hello. Jam and Butter Factory here. Can I help?'

Linda recognised the voice at the other end of the phone. It belonged to a lady called Mary whom she had talked with many times.

'Oh, hello, Mary. It's Linda in Tangmere. Please can you put me through to Colonel Sharp? Major Sheppard has an urgent message for him.'

'Certainly, Linda. Putting you through now.'

Soon the Major was connected to the Colonel.

'Failed to open? What is going on? Oh dear.' The Colonel was surprised at the news. 'Right. First, check with the parachute-makers. Tell them we cannot tolerate this happening any more. It's just far too often. Second, contact our agent in France who was going to meet with Sandra Eden and get them to look for the body. It would be best if the Germans didn't find her. Third, ensure her family get the requisite information regarding her death and, fourth, select an agent to take her place. Let me know who it is to be as soon as you have decided. Time is precious and we must act with all haste to cause as much disruption as possible in that region of France.'

'Yes, Sir. I will contact you as soon as the replacement agent is ready. Is that all?'

'Yes, all for now. Thank you, Major Sheppard.'

'Thank you, sir.'

Sheppard replaced the phone in its cradle and stared at the wall opposite while his mind took in all that had to be done. Who could take Sandra's place? There was no one quite like her, he thought. It was going to be a difficult task finding anyone to fill Sandra's shoes.

Sandra's family received information a couple of days later by telegram. It was a pre-printed note that said she was missing in action. Sandra's mum, Olivia, was shocked, devastated and beyond consolation. She prayed and prayed that Sandra might have been taken prisoner, but she knew from her contact with other unfortunate parents that 'missing in action' usually meant death. Sandra's dad, Jack, was in the Home Guard and he got the bad news from Olivia when he returned from duty that evening. He tried to console her as best he could in the circumstances. They both cried and prayed.

Major Sheppard had to work quickly to find a replacement for Sandra. He knew that an Allied invasion into France was very likely quite soon. The presence of thousands of American GIs everywhere pointed to some significant event in the near future. Sandra was to have operated in Normandy and it had been impressed on

Major Sheppard by his superiors that causing as much disruption as possible to enemy troop movements and communications was imperative. He had to find another agent who could be sent there and co-ordinate activity. Who could he choose? Two names came to mind: Nancy Lake and Barbara House. Both could speak French very well and Nancy had just completed SOE training in Scotland, while Barbara had recently returned from a secret teaching assignment in the United States. Either could do the job, yet only one was to go.

Major Sheppard reached into his pocket and pulled out a half-crown. Right, he thought, heads it's Nancy, tails it's Barbara, and tossed the coin into the air. It landed on the floor of his office and rolled under a chair. He bent down and looked under it. As he dragged the coin into view, King George VI stared blankly back. OK: it's Nancy Lake.

Sheppard reached for the phone on his desk and spoke to his secretary.

'Linda, put me through to Major Bishop at Cheltenham, please.'

'Yes, sir,' replied Linda.

Sheppard was quickly put through to the SOE training camp near Cheltenham, where he spoke to Bishop.

'Hello, Bob. Ed here. Something important has come up and I must have an agent here ASAP. Please will you send Nancy Lake on the next available train and tell her to report to Colonel Sharp in Baker Street as soon as she arrives? She will be told all that is necessary when she gets there.'

'Will do, Ed. I will make sure she's on the next train to Paddington. She should be in London before 6.30pm.'

'Thank you, Bob,' replied Sheppard.

In the tiny hamlet of Lynworth, immediately outside Cheltenham, where some SOE agents were camped awaiting orders, Nancy Lake was idling her time away and feeling very bored. She had spent several weeks training as an SOE agent and was ready for anything. She so wanted to do her bit.

The telephone in her room rang. It was Major Bishop.

'Nancy, I need to speak with you immediately. Come to my office.'

'Certainly, sir. Right away, sir.'

Nancy felt excited. Could this be what she had been waiting for?

She knocked and entered Bishop's office.

'Do sit down,' said Bishop, who proceeded to tell Nancy that she should collect her things and catch the train to Paddington.

'A car will take you to the station. It sounds as though you may well be off on an operation. I wish you all the very best of luck.'

'Have you no other information, sir?' This was the only response Nancy could think to give.

'No, none. But don't worry – you will be given all the necessary information in Baker Street. Thank you.'

Nancy saluted, said, 'Yes, sir,' and left the office.

The trip to London from Cheltenham Spa station took two hours, and from Paddington station Nancy took a taxi to Baker Street.

London looked miserable. Though it was only early evening, it was gloomy because of the rain. The taxi journey to SOE headquarters took longer than Nancy expected. This was mainly because of the twenty-mile-per-hour speed limit that had been introduced throughout London during the blackout to try to reduce the number of road casualties caused by the lack of light. Nancy thanked the driver for getting her there safely and, after paying for her journey, proceeded towards the main entrance of 64 Baker Street, where she was greeted by a uniformed secretary sitting at a desk just inside the main entrance.

'Can I be of assistance?' The secretary was very polite and gave Nancy a nice smile.

'Yes, please. My name is Nancy Lake and I've come to see Colonel Sharp. I believe he is stationed on the third floor.'

'Quite correct, but unfortunately he won't be in his office until 7am tomorrow. I can offer you a room across the hall for the night.'

'Yes, that would be helpful. Thank you.'

The secretary got up and showed Nancy the room where she would sleep that night. It was rather small, though comfortable. Nancy thanked the secretary and asked her to make sure she was woken at 6.30am. She then changed into her nightclothes and settled down in the bed. She was soon fast asleep.

The next morning saw Nancy dressed and ready for her interview in good time. She asked the secretary if it was possible to get breakfast in the building and was directed to the SOE dining room in the basement, where she was treated to a breakfast of eggs and bacon – something she had not had very often since rationing was introduced at the start of the war.

'My, you are very lucky to have access to such a lovely breakfast!' she said to the uniformed officer sat opposite her.

'You're right. It is one of the few benefits for those who work here. But I imagine you are just passing through?'

'Possibly. I will soon find out.'

Nancy said 'Cheerio' to the officer and took her plate and

cutlery back to the collecting place adjacent to the kitchen. She then walked upstairs to the ground floor and approached the secretary's desk.

'Ah, Miss Lake. Please would you go to the Colonel's office on the third floor. It is clearly marked. He is waiting for you.'

'Thank you,' said Nancy.

Colonel Sharp's office was spacious with a window that overlooked Baker Street.

'Please sit down, Miss Lake. We have much to discuss.'

Nancy sat facing the Colonel who said, 'You have been chosen for this operation on the basis of your command of French and your very good reports from SOE training centres. Indeed, the comments received from our trainers put you in the top tier of new agents. I won't beat about the bush. You have to know that this is not going to be easy, but it is of vital importance to the Allies. The area that you will be sent to in France is near Normandy and your job will be to contact the French Resistance Maquis leaders there, who will help you in your efforts to cause as much disruption to the enemy as you can. All the targets and contact names will be given to you this afternoon during your briefing. You will be leaving tonight by Lysander from Tangmere airfield. The 5pm train from Waterloo will get you there in time. Any questions?'

'Yes. Will the Lysander be landing, or will I be making a parachute drop?'

'Parachute drop. It's the safest way to get you there. The Germans would have a greater chance of capturing you if the plane lands.'

'I see,' said Nancy.

'Right. Now report to Sergeant Bligh in the briefing room

at 1pm. He will be waiting for you and will give you all the information and supplies you need. Good luck.'

Nancy was surprised to be given two words of encouragement at the end. She stood up, saluted and said, 'Yes, sir', then left the office.

Sergeant Bligh was a large imposing figure with a deep voice. He asked Nancy to sit down and, after going through the codes and location of her operation, said, 'There is one thing you must know. The SOE agent Sandra Eden was your predecessor on this operation. She was parachuted into Normandy one week ago. However, unfortunately her parachute did not open. The pilot of the Lysander watched as she plummeted to her death. But for that you would not be here. We have no word on what happened to her body, but we are hoping the Germans did not find her because if they did, they would know what she was and may well try and put an imposter in her place to mislead us. Please be aware of this just in case. Any questions?'

'No. But thank you for all this information. I will read and memorise some of it now, then I'll be off to catch the train from Waterloo at 5pm.'

Bligh said, 'Before you go, the Colonel needs to speak to you.'

The wireless operator in Baker Street handed the message received from Normandy station N4 to her superior officer, Lieutenant George. He read the message, then went from his office to see his commander.

'Message from N4, sir.' He handed the piece of paper to Brigadier Royal, who read through it slowly.

'What this says is that Sandra Eden is alive, and we know that is not true. The Germans must have found her body and are trying to fool us. Get me Colonel Sharp, urgently,' he said.

Sharp was soon sitting in Royal's office.

'We have received a message claiming that Sandra Eden is alive,' said Brigadier Royal. 'Now we know that she died when her parachute didn't open, but the Germans must have some of her information and codes. They must have found her body and made all the usual deductions. This could have bad consequences for the Maquis in the area. We must get the replacement agent there as soon as possible in order that she calm things down with the Maquis and set our plans into operation. When is she going?'

'She is in the briefing room as we speak, sir.'

'And how does she seem to you? Will she make a good job of it?'

Sharp was surprised at Royal's question. All SOE agents were exceptional in his eyes. Their training was designed to ensure only the best got through.

'Yes, sir. She is more than up to the job, I'm sure.'

'Good. Now I think you should let her know what happened to Sandra Eden before she goes. It is as well she is aware of it. She needs all possible information we can give her before she meets the Maquis and begins her task. Is she parachuting into France?'

'Yes, sir, and she is probably being told about Sandra as we speak.'

'Good. Let me know when she is safely in France.'

'Yes, sir.' Sharp saluted and left Royal's office.

Sharp was soon on his way to the briefing room. When he entered, he saw Nancy sitting at a desk reading from a book of codes, surrounded by the bits and pieces of equipment she would be taking with her to France that very evening.

Nancy stood up and saluted as Sharp entered the room. Sergeant Bligh did likewise.

'Please sit down. I have something to tell you. We have received a message from one of the Maquis agents in France claiming that Sandra Eden is alive. We know that she must be dead – her parachute did not open when she was sent to France a few days ago. No one could have survived her fall. I want you to know that if you meet anyone who claims to be her, they will almost certainly be a German agent. Once you have satisfied yourself that you are being misled, shoot them! Do I make myself clear?'

'Yes, sir. Of course. Thank you.'

Nancy went to Waterloo station, where she caught the train to Chichester. A car picked her up at the station and took her the short distance to the airfield, where she was soon fully kitted out with a parachute and all the necessary equipment required. An RAF pilot walked into the room where Nancy had just put on her chute.

'How do you do? My name is James. James Silverstone. I will be your pilot for this evening.'

Nancy was impressed. This chap seemed to exude confidence and he was very handsome. It would have been nice to get to know him, but she knew it would be impossible at that time.

'Nancy Lake. Pleased to meet you. When are we going?'

'My orders are to leave in about twenty minutes. As soon as you are ready, we can walk from here to my plane.'

'OK. Let's make a go of it!'

They both walked across to where the Lysander was waiting for them and boarded.

James asked, 'Are you all strapped in?'

'All strapped in and ready to go!'

'Good,' said James. 'Now hang on to your hat – and the very best of luck.'

With that, James fired up the Bristol Mercury engine that powered the Lysander and began taxiing down the runway. Quietly to himself, he said a prayer for Nancy's safety.

James put the engine on full throttle and leaned back in his seat as the Lysander sped down the runway. The wheels were very soon off the ground.

'We're off!' he said into his intercom.

Nancy was on her way to Normandy.

Chapter 2

The blackness around Sandra was all-enveloping. As she fell, she could not think of anything other than, 'Damn you, damn you! Open! Open!' as she pulled and pulled at the ripcord. 'Please open, please open!'

It was no good. Her useless parachute was streaming upwards and was not going to open properly. It was just a hopeless strip of white silk. She realised this was it: she was going to die. Damn! What a way to go, after all she'd been through to get here. This feeling of utter helplessness overwhelmed her as she tumbled through the black night towards the ground, and towards death. How much longer – five seconds? Ten seconds? What could she do? Nothing. She tried to brace herself for the collision with the earth. This was not how she wanted to die. Damn those bloody Nazis! Damn this bloody parachute! All her family and friends – she would never see them again. Never. Her life was gone. Everything was gone. Why?

She felt the ground hit the back of her legs…at least, she thought it was the ground. Everything was happening at super-speed and she expected her whole, rather short, life to flash before her eyes immediately. It didn't happen. The ground gave way. Yes, gave way! Then her back and neck felt the ground – and that gave way, too. What was happening? Then her whole body felt the ground, and again it gave way. It was not the ground. She was slowing up! Something was cushioning her fall, but what?

She continued falling, but more and more slowly, and then she realised what was happening. She had hit a tree. Its branches were breaking and bending around her as she fell through them. They just kept breaking as her body crashed towards the earth. Then she stopped falling and hit the wet ground with a thump that knocked the wind from her lungs, her head spinning and arms and legs aching from all the contact with the now broken branches that had saved her – yes, saved her. She was alive. Thank God!

Sandra lay there under her saviour tree – breathless and exhausted, she couldn't move. The rain washed her face as she took deep breaths and tried to feel all the parts of her body to make sure nothing was broken. Had she really survived? Jumping from 3,000 feet with only a faulty parachute for company? Yes! She turned over on the ground and could feel bruises and aches all over her body. But they were as nothing because she was alive. She crawled on her stomach towards the trunk of the protector tree, then curled up in a ball to feel safer. She must have lain there, unmoving, for twenty or thirty minutes, gradually becoming more aware of her astonishing good fortune and becoming more rain-soaked.

She eventually forced herself into a sitting position, with her back resting against the tree trunk. The thought that came to mind at that time was, 'If you can survive this, you can survive anything!' But where were her contacts? Would they have seen her falling? Surely, they would have seen the plane, even if she was not visible due to the lack of an open parachute. She must have landed near the planned rendezvous location. Where were they?

As she lay there, slowly recovering from the shock of the fall, the rain ceased and the first glimmers of light came into the sky as the sun began to rise. She started to feel that she ought to try to stand up and attempt to move to a place of greater safety. Her efforts were interrupted by the sound of movement and footsteps nearby. She reached for her pistol.

'*Qu'avons-nous ici?*' ('What have we here?')

The voice was on the left. She turned towards it.

'*Le vent vient-il de l'est?*' ('Is the wind from the east?')

'*Non, c'est de l'ouest,*' she replied. ('No, it is from the west.')

The Frenchman who had addressed Sandra was apprehensively looking down at her bedraggled state. But now they knew they were friends, having exchanged the planned greeting to be used when first meeting. She released the grip on the pistol and extended her hand towards him.

'Sandra Eden, at your service.' He gripped her hand and shook it.

'Captain Michel Tardivat, at yours, and what happened to your chute?'

'It didn't open. I don't know how I survived. The tree broke my fall. It saved me.'

'*Mon Dieu!!* Are you joking?'

'No, I am not joking. Please help me up.'

The Captain pulled her to her feet. At the same time, another Frenchman, who introduced himself as Marcel, came up alongside the Captain and helped him position Sandra in an upright position resting against the tree. The useless chute was still attached to her and together they removed it.

Holding the parachute up and looking at it, the Captain said, 'Well, you really are a very fortunate woman. This tree must be well over thirty metres high, and with so many branches! God really must have held you in his hands.'

Sandra could feel all her sensations returning. She was sure she could walk now and was certain there were no broken bones – just lots of bruises. Yes, she was very lucky. A miraculous escape.

'Thank you, Captain. Please could you take me to your safe house? I need to change my clothes and get warm. We have lots to discuss.'

'Of course. It's about two kilometres from here. But please call me Michel. And may I say that I hope all the trees in France bear such beautiful fruit as you this year.'

'Thank you, but there is no need for that French *merde*! Come on, let's go.'

She was helped by the two of them through the forest, then on to open ground where they could see the old farmhouse. She managed to walk a little, but was very aware of the extensive bruises, aches and pains over most of her body. Eventually they reached the safe house. Sandra was almost out on her feet, exhausted. She was taken inside and made to lie down. She was too weary even to change her clothes, which were drying out slowly anyway. Marcel made a drink that tasted like coffee, which was very welcome and the first coffee she had tasted in a very long time. Her mind was in a bit of turmoil after the events of the last few hours, but she was eager to get started on her task.

'When can I meet your Maquis group leader?' she asked. 'I need to understand the organisation's construction and plan its activities. The next few weeks are very important.'

'You must rest first. Please try and sleep now. When you are better, we will arrange a meeting.'

She knew Michel was right, but as always, she just wanted to get on and get things done. She decided to allow her tiredness to overcome her and eventually fell asleep.

She was awoken by much pain as once again she became aware of the aches and bruises from the fall. According to Michel, she had been asleep for only a few hours. He was still in the room, watching over her. She forced herself to move slowly as she blinked her way to consciousness.

'How do you feel?' Michel was nothing if not considerate.

'In agony, pure agony,' she croaked.

'Well, it is better than the alternative,' was the blunt response.

'Alternative? What do you mean?'

'Death.'

'Oh. Oh yes, of course.' He was right. 'Have you got my cigarettes?' she asked.

'I put all your things in that pile on the table. I'll get them for you.'

Michel rummaged in the pile of belongings that had come down with Sandra from the Lysander and produced a pack of twenty Senior Service cigarettes, which he handed to her. She was not a heavy smoker – a pack of twenty would last for four or five days – yet she felt a strong need for a cigarette now to help her calm down. Michel offered a lighted match and she took a deep draw. She offered him one, but he declined.

'What are your objectives for this visit?' asked Michel.

'Many and varied,' Sandra replied. 'I will need to meet your Maquis leaders and co-ordinate a number of actions. It is imperative that we disrupt the German operations in this area as much and as soon as possible. I will expect our attacks to target rail links, roads and communications.'

'How will you do that? We are very short of supplies, especially bomb-making material.'

'That shouldn't be too much of a problem. Just let me know what supplies you need, and I will arrange the necessaries to be parachuted in from London – though let's hope the parachutes they use will open this time! Make a list of what you require quickly, because there really isn't much time available.'

Michel took out a pen and proceeded to write down a rather long list of items. She began feeling better, mainly because things were moving in the right direction. She had been given very clear plans by her SOE commander before leaving for France. The Nazi communication links around the Normandy area must be disrupted as soon as possible. She had to get things going!

The next morning, Sandra felt different, mainly because she had actually managed to sleep very well – for at least six hours. Her mind was still working overtime and was impatient to meet the Maquis. The plan had been outlined in London to destroy many train links in and around Normandy. This would mean the use of large amounts of explosive and the organising of at least four separate groups of Maquis, so that the sabotage operations could all happen at similar times and maximise the disruption it would cause.

Breakfast was good – at least better than what she had become used to back home. They had eggs, bacon and mushrooms. It was heaven! Well, she was on a farm and imagined that those who lived here were familiar with this fare most days.

Sandra looked across at Michel and said, 'Michel, I must outline my first plan of operation to you. Please can we go to another room with your maps? I'll tell you what is required.'

'Of course. Let's go next door. All we need is in there. We can leave Claudette to clear our breakfast things away.'

Claudette was the farmer's wife who had been so very helpful when they arrived the previous evening. Nothing seemed too much trouble for her. She knew just a few words of English, but they managed to get on well – mainly because of Sandra's ability with the French language, which had been learned during many years living in Paris with her parents in the 1930s. She loved the French people and enjoyed Paris, not least because of the nightlife there, which she had become very used to as a young woman.

The room they entered had a large table in the middle with plenty of chairs positioned around it. Michel spread the maps across the table, and they sat together and examined them closely. Sandra pointed to the Gare de Lisieux, a railway station situated near Caen, and said, 'There. That's it. That's where we must concentrate our efforts and hopefully destroy all – and I do mean all – the lines both into and out of the station. When can I meet your men and arrange an attack?'

Michel looked thoughtful and replied, 'I have arranged for two of them to meet us here this afternoon. I suggest we don't meet more than two at any one time – it's just too dangerous. We can co-ordinate their activities as a group, but we must not compromise the action by risking us all getting together at the same time in the same place.'

She agreed with him. They then discussed the various tactics to be employed. The priority was the destruction of the railway links between Gare de Lisieux and the area on the eastern side of Normandy. Michel knew where the lines were least protected, and they soon formulated a plan that should destroy the two major links. It involved blowing up large sections of railway in order that they could not be repaired quickly by the Germans.

The two members of the Maquis were due to arrive at 1pm. She was looking forward to outlining the plan to them and getting their views on its feasibility.

Charles and Henri arrived on time and the four of them sat down around a bale of hay in the barn. It was best not to meet in the farmhouse in case they compromised Claudette and her husband. Sandra began by introducing herself in French, which seemed to please them, but the ensuing conversation was in English as she discovered they could both understand it.

'Thank you both for coming here,' she said, 'though in future we'd better limit our meetings and change our meeting places regularly to minimise the risk of capture.'

They both nodded their assent.

'Can I assume that you are both Maquis commanders?'

Charles responded, 'Yes, yes, we are both commanders. Together we control up to 100 men. What are your plans for us? And can you get us some guns and ammunition? We are short of almost everything necessary to continue our resistance to the Nazis.'

Sandra replied, 'I can certainly try to obtain what you require. First, I'll need to contact London. Michel will help with that. I know he has access to a wireless and he's told me what he thinks you'll need, but give me a list of any other requirements and we'll send it on to London. They will parachute the supplies to us. But first I need to explain my proposed plans to you. You are both here and know the area very well, I expect. Let's look at the map.'

Sandra produced a map of the area from her satchel and spread it over the hay bale. On it were marked some strategic points on roads and railways that were pointed out to Charles and Henri. They looked on with great interest.

'Where and when do you intend to start operations?' asked Henri.

'The first target is going to be the Sainte-Catherine tunnel. It is an important link between Rouen and Caen. If we can disable it for a few weeks, it will prevent or at least slow down supplies to German troops in the area around Caen and Bayeux. So, I think this would be a good start.'

'Will not be easy,' said Henri. 'The Germans know how important the tunnel is and would want to repair any damage quickly. Besides, they will have it well guarded. There is also the possibility that, if successful, targeting such an important link might result in reprisals. The Germans would not hesitate to prevent further attacks by killing innocent people in the surrounding villages.'

Sandra looked at Henri and said, 'Yes. I've been thinking about that possibility, but we can't afford the luxury of doing nothing. If we do not help in some way to assist the coming invasion, who knows what the future holds?'

'Coming invasion? Do you know something?'

Michel was becoming intrigued. The fact that Sandra was there and seemed to have quite explicit plans for disruption was good, but did she know more?

'No. I know nothing. Only what my superiors in London have told me, which is what you see in front of you on this map. They want these targets sabotaged urgently. That is all I know.'

'Sounds good to me,' said Charles. 'Let's compile this list of things that you can get for us. Yes?'

'Yes,' she agreed.

The four of them spent the next few minutes thinking aloud while Sandra wrote down all the supplies that were required, which included explosives, detonators, guns and ammunition. After the list was completed, it was handed to Michel.

'Well, thank you both for being so helpful. We will let London know what we need and I'm sure they will get these things over to us quickly. I suggest we meet elsewhere soon to discuss when to make our attack.'

'Will you be helping us blow up the tunnel? It will be very dangerous, especially for a woman.' Henri looked concerned as he said this.

Sandra suppressed her irritation and answered, rather pointedly, 'Helping you? I shall be leading you!'

After Charles and Henri left the barn, Michel took the list given to him into the farmhouse. He climbed the stairs to the small bedroom and, once inside, collected the wireless he used to contact London. He never used it in the farmhouse. He always went somewhere in the surrounding woods to send a message. This, he knew, was a safer way of sending and receiving messages as the Germans would be unable to permanently fix exactly where they were being sent from. Once Michel had sent the message, together with the code Sandra had given him, he returned to the farmhouse.

Shutting the farmhouse door, he said, 'London did respond with just a short despatch of two separate messages. The first was, "The painting is on the wall." Do you know what that means?'

She knew exactly what it meant. It was one of the short coded messages that had been drummed into her before leaving London. The code meant that London would be back in contact with a time and place to drop the supplies they had requested. That was encouraging to know.

'That's good. We should get a time and place for the drop next time you contact them. Will you do just that tomorrow night?'

'Yes, of course. And in the meantime we can plan in detail how to blow up the tunnel.'

Sandra nodded. Things were beginning to go as she had hoped.

'Oh, and what was the second message?'

'"The price of butter is coming down." What does that mean?'

'That means another agent is to be parachuted here this evening. I will meet them and liaise. Can you take me back to where you found me in the forest in good time? The drop will probably take place sometime between 10pm and midnight. I can't think why they are sending another agent, but it will be good to find out.'

Later that evening, Sandra and Michel left their hideaway in the farmyard barn and proceeded to the drop zone. The walk was about a mile and a quarter and it would take about twenty-five minutes to get through the woods to the open area where the drop would take place. Michel led the way through the darkness. There was only a little light from the three-quarter moon, but he knew where they were going. He had been this way many times before.

Eventually, they reached the open field and busied themselves laying out the markers to guide the plane. They would light them just before the time they expected the agent to land. They had to keep the time the markers were alight to a minimum to avoid attracting undue attention. The Gestapo were aware that the Allies were making drops of agents and supplies, and were continually monitoring large areas of the countryside to try to detect any activity.

'It's almost 10pm. Time to light the markers,' said Sandra.

'Yes, let's do it now,' agreed Michel.

Together they ran down the field lighting the small markers that were arranged in a letter 'L'. Having completed that task, they returned to a spot at the edge of the field where they were hidden by the woods. It was then that they heard the sound of a plane.

'There it is!' exclaimed Michel. 'It must have spotted our markers.'

The Lysander could now be seen just ahead of where they were hiding. They did not have to wait long before they saw what they were expecting. A parachute opened and floated slowly down towards the letter 'L'.

'Well, at least the bloody parachute works!' commented Sandra, who was relieved to see it open after her own recent experience.

'Come on. Let's go and collect the agent quickly and put out the lights.'

They sprinted across the field to where the parachute had just landed, extinguishing the markers on their way. Michel made sure they were all put out, while Sandra approached the parachutist, who was partially wrapped in white silk and trying to get the chute under control.

'*Qu'avons-nous ici?*' ('What have we here?') Sandra asked.

'*Le vent vient-il de l'est?*' ('Is the wind from the east?') replied the figure wrapped in silk.

'*Non, c'est de l'ouest.*' ('No, it is from the west.')

Sandra was more than a little surprised to discover the agent was a woman. After their exchange of coded messages confirmed they were friends, she said, 'Let me help you with your chute, and please follow me. We must get into the forest as quickly as possible.'

Michel was soon back with them and they ran into the forest, where they stopped for a moment to gather their breath.

Nancy was glad of the pause. It gave her time to draw breath and introduce herself. By now she had collected her parachute into a small bundle and had her backpack slung over her shoulder.

'I'm Nancy Lake. Very pleased to meet you both,' she said as she extended her hand towards Sandra and Michel.

'Captain Michel Tardivat, at your service.'

'And I'm Sandra Eden. Nice to meet you. Glad you had a safe landing.'

Nancy did not respond to Sandra's greeting. She bent over her backpack and fumbled inside it for a few seconds. When she stood up, she stepped away from Sandra and Michel and held up her pistol, pointing it at both of them.

'Don't move. I won't hesitate to shoot.'

Sandra was shocked. Michel looked askance at Nancy and said, 'What are you doing? We're here to help you! Stop being so silly.'

'I'm not being silly. You are. We know Sandra Eden is dead. She was seen, by the pilot of the Lysander I have just jumped from, plunging to her death when her parachute didn't open. You are no more Sandra Eden than I am. She's dead, and you must both be German spies. Say your prayers!'

'Wait! You are mistaken. She survived!' Michel held out his hands as he pleaded with Nancy.

His words had some effect on her as she didn't pull the trigger. 'Survived? How?'

'I'll tell you how,' said Sandra, 'but please listen. I really do not want to be shot by one of my own people.'

'Make it quick – and it had better be pretty convincing because I don't want to be captured by some nasty Nazi spies.'

'Of course you don't. We are all in this together. I survived because I landed off-target among some trees, which cushioned my fall as I fell through the branches. They slowed me up enough to save me before I hit the ground. Hard to believe? Yes, I guess it is. But true.'

'I can vouch for that. I reached Sandra soon after she landed. Her chute was useless, but thankfully she was alive. It was a miracle. You must believe us.' Michel advanced slightly towards Nancy as he spoke.

She immediately pointed her pistol straight at his chest and shouted, 'Don't move! Stay where you are!'

Nancy was in a dilemma. How could she be sure that Sandra had survived? The story they told was just short of unbelievable.

How could anyone live after falling so far with no parachute? She thought of a question.

'Tell me the name of your pilot in the Lysander.'

Sandra smiled and said, 'Flight Lieutenant James Silverstone. I met him just before we took off. He seemed such a nice chap. He must still be flying if he piloted you over here from England.'

'Yes, he is. Now tell me what he looks like.'

'Well, that's a difficult one. I only saw him for a short while before he put on his helmet and we took off, but if I had to compare him to anyone I'd say he had the dark handsome looks of Laurence Olivier.'

Nancy was satisfied with that answer. She had thought the same.

'Right. That will do,' she said as she replaced her pistol in its holster. She knew there was really no way a German imposter could know just how handsome James Silverstone looked or would compare him to Laurence Olivier. Only a red-blooded lady from the Empire could have matched them so well.

Michel and Sandra breathed sighs of relief. Sandra embraced Nancy and said, 'Thank you. Thank you. But does London really believe I am dead? Have they told my family?'

'Yes, afraid so. Silverstone saw the Roman Candle as your chute failed and reported back that you must have died. That's why I'm here. You must tell me more about surviving such a drop. What a miracle! And we must let London know you are alive, though that might be difficult. They may even think I've been compromised in some way. We need to sit down and give this plenty of thought. Talking of sitting down, how about we get moving? You can take me to the safe house and we can perhaps have a cup of something while we decide exactly what to do.'

'Good idea. Let's go.' With that, Michel led them through the woods towards the farmhouse. They soon reached it and, after making sure it was safe to enter, went in and sat in the kitchen. Both Claudette and her husband, Patrice, welcomed them in and offered them coffee, which they gratefully accepted. They were so glad to be alive after all that had occurred. Claudette and Patrice left them to discuss their plans and went off to bed. It was getting rather late and they had their usual early start in the morning to keep the farm running. They wished each other *'Bonne nuit.'*

Michel was sitting between the two women at the kitchen table. He found it unusual to be surrounded by two female agents from England. He had been involved in the Resistance since the Nazis had overrun most of France and Sandra was the first female agent he had encountered. Now there were two! He was the first to speak.

'I consider it a priority that I contact London to tell them Sandra is alive and that you, Nancy, have arrived safely. They may want to change plans based on the new situation. What do you think?'

Nancy said, 'Good idea. My orders are to organise the Maquis in this area to destroy a number of communication links and blow up the aircraft factory at Caudebec-en-Caux that manufactures parts for German Luftwaffe bombers and fighters. I guess this would be similar to the orders given to you, Sandra, before you came over?'

'Similar, yes. But not the factory. There must be a good reason why that has been added. Surely that could be left to the RAF to destroy?'

'Exactly what I thought when they told me,' said Nancy.

'Then why do they want us to do it?'

'Well, the reasons they gave me included the fact the RAF have tried already with limited success, and they think a plan involving the Maquis will limit the number of French civilian casualties, especially workers in the factory. It does make sense, don't you think?'

Michel said, 'The attack on the factory will be difficult. We will need many men and explosives. London will have to send us a lot of arms and equipment. We must also be prepared to suffer some losses of men. The factory is very well defended by German troops. We would have to work quickly to surprise them. The last thing we want to face would be a pitched battle with their troops.'

'Agreed,' said Sandra. 'That attack will require careful planning. First, let's deal with the railway communication links, especially the tunnel at Sainte-Catherine. We should be able to block that quickly.'

'Why not tomorrow evening? We have enough explosives to do the job. Let's do it!'

Nancy was nothing if not enthusiastic.

'Why not? It will only take two of us to enter the tunnel, plant the explosives and get away. We could do it together.' Sandra was looking at Nancy as she said this.

The response was immediate. 'Done! Just show me where the tunnel is and we will do it. Tomorrow night around 10pm. Is that OK?'

Michel was slightly taken aback. Two women agreeing to carry out this act of sabotage! This was unusual in his experience. He was slightly in awe of the two of them. They were utterly fearless. He was unsure what to say, but suggested anyway, 'Perhaps I could accompany you both and help with planting the explosives? I would not expect there to be any Nazi troops guarding the tunnel entrances. It is in quite a remote location some ten miles from here. But you never know.'

'Thank you for that,' said Sandra, 'but we will manage on our own. There is no need for you to risk your life. We're both familiar with the use of explosives. We have had some very good training in England.'

'So true,' said Nancy, 'but thank you anyway. And if there are any German troops around, we will deal with them. Have no fear.'

Michel was struck by the determination they both showed, especially Nancy, who seemed to radiate daring. She was quite a woman, he thought.

'Very well. I will guide you to the tunnel tomorrow night and leave you to travel the last mile on your own. I will wait for your return, then we can make our way back here.'

'Thank you,' said Nancy. 'Now, is there anything to drink?'

'You mean more coffee?' asked Michel.

'Coffee? Coffee? Do me a favour! I have been looking forward to trying some French wine for weeks! There isn't any in England, but I'm told you have it for breakfast over here.' Nancy laughed.

'Well. Not quite for breakfast. I think there may be some Calvados brandy somewhere around.' With that, Michel stood up and went towards a small cupboard in the corner of the kitchen. After some rummaging, he produced the bottle of Calvados. It was half-full and quickly consumed with much appreciation, mostly by Nancy. The evening was drawing to a close.

'Time for bed,' said Sandra. 'Nancy, you can sleep in my

room in the outhouse. There is a spare mattress.'

Michel said goodbye and left them. He would return to his house in the village and they would all meet again the following night. He planned to send their agreed message to London before he went to bed.

Michel contacted London on his way back. He was in the woods at a place he had not used to send messages before. When he was connected, he told them Sandra was alive and asked for more arms, ammunition and explosives to be sent in order to carry out the sabotage. After receiving confirmation from London, he packed the wireless away in its small suitcase and hid it in its waterproof lair on his way home. Michel thought about the two female agents he was to work alongside. A completely new experience for him. This was an interesting time!

Chapter 3

The following evening Sandra and Nancy were all prepared for their operation when Michel arrived to collect them and lead them to the tunnel at Sainte-Catherine. They walked through the woods in single file. There was a half-moon that night though it was cloudy which made it rather dark, but Michel knew the way very well. After some three hours of walking, he called a halt and gave Sandra and Nancy directions for the last mile to the tunnel. He would then wait for them to return and lead them back to the farmhouse. He wished them '*bonne chance.*'

Together Sandra and Nancy made their way through the woods towards the tunnel. They reached the entrance within twenty minutes of leaving Michel and, having made sure there were no German soldiers keeping guard, they climbed down the railway embankment and entered the tunnel. It was rather dark and smelled damp and musty inside. They slowly made their way forward for about a minute, using Nancy's torch to guide them, until they were well inside.

Sandra stopped, took her backpack from her shoulder and said, 'Let's plant our explosives here. We are close enough to the entrance to get out in good time.'

'Good idea,' replied Nancy.

Together they planted their explosives in the wall of the tunnel on both sides of the railway tracks. When they had finished, Nancy turned to Sandra and said, 'All ready here.'

Sandra was about to reply when their conversation was interrupted by the distant rumble of a train.

'Quick, switch off the torch!' cried Sandra. 'And push yourself against the wall. There isn't much room in here.'

The distant rumble had become a roar as the train came closer to where they were stuck in the tunnel.

The speed of the train and its proximity to her body made Sandra press her back to the tunnel wall as hard as she possibly could. There were just a few inches between her face and the train as it hurtled through the tunnel on its way to Le Havre. It was difficult to breathe properly as the air felt like it was being sucked from her lungs. And then came the relief as the train passed by, leaving that huge empty space behind full of smoke, steam and the smell of oil. She could breathe better now.

'Well, that was a close shave! Let's get on with it. Pass me the pencil detonator.'

Sandra spoke through the darkness to Nancy, who had been fortunate enough to position herself on the other side of the tunnel when the train passed and consequently did not experience its proximity inches from her body. Instead, there had been a whole extra track-width of safety between her and the train.

'Yes, a close shave for you definitely! Here's the detonator,' Nancy said, handing it to Sandra. 'Be careful – it is quite sensitive.'

Sandra didn't need reminding just how sensitive these detonators were. She had experience of using them during her SOE training in Scotland.

'Yes, of course. Now how long will it take us to get out of this tunnel to safety? What do you reckon? Say, five minutes?'

'That sounds reasonable. Yes. Set the detonator to go after five minutes.'

'No, I'll set it for ten minutes. We will be able to watch the whole thing go up from the hill opposite. There will be less chance of anyone seeing us near the explosion when it happens.'

'Right. Let's do it.'

Sandra set the detonator in the forty pounds of explosive they had crammed into the tunnel wall and activated it.

'Let's go. Quick!'

They began running carefully along the track towards the tunnel entrance. They reached it without mishap well within five minutes and stopped to ensure there was no one nearby to see them come out.

Sandra looked around and said, 'C'mon, let's climb up the embankment and wait over there behind that tree. Follow me.'

Nancy followed in Sandra's wake as she climbed up the grassy slope. They kept going for a few minutes, then stopped near the tree where they could see the tunnel, and waited. Only the sound of night – owls hooting nearby – accompanied their short wait.

When it came, the explosion in the tunnel was much muffled. A few seconds later, smoke billowed from the tunnel entrance, signifying the success of their plan. There was no way of knowing what would happen to the next train through the tunnel, but it would almost certainly crash to a stop, and they were not going to wait around to witness it. They turned away and made their way towards the place where Michel had left them. Keeping themselves well hidden in the trees surrounding them, they took about half an hour to reach the relative safety of the place where Michel was waiting.

'How did it go?' asked Michel.

'Very well. We would say the tunnel is now blocked,' said Sandra, 'though we did have a narrow escape when a train came through as we were setting the explosives. But we survived.'

'Good work! You are both wonders to behold.' They were heroes in his eyes!

The three of them made their way through the woods and the night, again led by Michel. By the time they reached the safety of the farmhouse, it was almost 5am. A long night!

They entered the kitchen. It was Nancy who spoke first. 'How about a drink? Have you got any more Calvados?'

Michel managed to find another bottle in a cupboard in the corner of the kitchen.

Nancy was of a mind to celebrate what she and Sandra had just achieved, and there was no disagreement from the others. Michel poured each of them a glass.

'Ooh, I do like the taste. It's so nice and sweet!' Nancy was obviously beginning to enjoy herself and the three of them were soon in a good mood, fortified by the effects of the sweet brandy of Normandy. They decided they would celebrate their success for as long as they could. It had been a difficult operation with an effective outcome. The only hindrance to celebrating for a long time was the scarcity of Calvados. There was only three-quarters of a bottle, and that did not go very far or last very long.

Later that morning, Nancy sent a message to London using Michel's wireless transmitter. She detailed the success of the tunnel explosion and reiterated the fact that Sandra was alive. She wanted to know, of course, what London wanted her to do now. The answer to that question would come later.

Sure enough, that evening Michel returned from another safe house some distance from the farm where he had been in contact with London. He read out the message he'd received, which was that Nancy was to go to Paris, contact other agents there and prepare for what they hoped would soon arrive: the liberation of Paris by the Allies.

Nancy listened to Michel in silence. She was not surprised. After all, she had only been sent here to replace Sandra and that was now unnecessary. Besides, on the positive side, a visit to Paris would be nice, bringing back memories of when she lived there with her mother. However, she was rather disappointed because she had much enjoyed being with Sandra and would miss her.

'Sorry you'll be leaving us,' said Sandra.

'Me too,' was the reply.

'When have you got to go?'

'As soon as I am packed up. I will catch the train. There is a direct one from the local station. I'll go tomorrow.'

'Let me help you pack,' offered Sandra, and the two of them

went to the kitchen to prepare Nancy for her new adventure.

Early the following morning, Nancy and Sandra walked to the railway station where Nancy would catch the early train to Paris. The station entrance was guarded by German soldiers and Sandra said her goodbyes to Nancy without getting too close. Nancy approached the entrance and the guard demanded to see her identification papers. She handed them over with a smile and, after quickly reading them, he handed them back. They worked! Thank goodness, thought Nancy, who was soon on the train to Paris. Fortunately, the route the train took did not go anywhere near the tunnel she had helped destroy the previous day!

After leaving Nancy, Sandra met with a Maquis agent nearby. His name was Julian and she had been introduced to him previously by Michel. Following the plan told to her by Nancy, she told him to make arrangements for the secret delivery of explosives to an aircraft factory. This was an important part of the plan to destroy the factory. After the meeting with Julian, Sandra returned to the safe house where she was due to meet Michel and others from the Maquis to explain the plans for sabotage. It was going to be a very interesting meeting.

When Sandra arrived at the barn next to the safe house, only Michel was there. He had arranged for four Maquis leaders to meet them to discuss tactics. They knew meeting in such a comparatively large group was not the best thing to do. But Sandra wanted to talk to the four leaders at the same time so they would all get the same message, in spite of the risk involved. They were due to arrive at 2pm and there was still ten minutes to go. Sandra and Michel quickly went through an outline of the presentation and agreed that they were ready to deliver it to the Maquis.

The four Maquis leaders arrived at different times, but all within ten minutes of each other. Charles and Henri were the first to arrive, closely followed by Alphonse and Louis, who were introduced to Sandra by Michel. All five Maquis knew each other and seemed to Sandra to be on good terms. After a few minutes exchanging greetings, they sat down on hay bales and waited for Sandra to begin. She smiled at them.

'Firstly, thank you for coming here at such short notice, and my apologies if any of you find it difficult to understand what I am saying. Please let me know if anything is unclear and Michel will explain my message for you. Secondly, this is a very important time in the fight to overcome the Nazis. We can expect an Allied invasion some time, and when it comes it will be our job to cause as much interference to Nazi troop movements as possible. That is why you are here now. I have plans to destroy an armaments factory and other important targets crucial to our success.'

At this point, Sandra produced her map and spread it out on a couple of hay bales. 'Gather round. Let me show you here what we have to do.'

The men gathered around the map and began pointing at the different places shown on it, all of which were familiar to them.

'Now then, the first target I want you to be looking at is the aircraft factory at Caudebec-en-Caux. You all know it, I'm sure. It is a major source of aircraft components for the German air force. We need to knock it out. We will do this by infiltrating the site, planting some explosives at strategic places all around the factory and blowing it to kingdom come after we have all got out and away from the area. The place is guarded, but I want this job done without a full-frontal assault. We have to plant the explosives without arousing suspicion.'

'Why can't the RAF bombers do it? It would save us a lot of trouble and they would probably do a more thorough job.' The interruption came from Alphonse, who was looking at Sandra intently.

'They tried that three weeks ago. It had little effect and many of the bombs fell where they should not have, causing a number of civilian casualties. Apart from everything else, it was not good for morale. London have made their decision and it now falls to us to do the job properly. Any other questions?'

'Yes. When do you want us to do this, and how are we to gain access to the factory without setting off alarms?'

'We will all be disguised as workers, so we should be able to gain access with the minimum of trouble. Later, I will tell you when we will do this.'

'How are we to smuggle explosives into the factory? Surely the workers are searched regularly by German security. It will be impossible to carry lots of explosives through the factory gates without risking immediate detection.' Louis said this with a quizzical look at Sandra.

'That's true. And that's why we won't be carrying any explosives into the factory. The explosives will be delivered to the main gate hidden within a batch of engine components. They will be stored in the usual locations and we will access them when needed and prime them to explode.'

When Sandra had finished speaking, Louis, who had stood up, remarked, 'Well, that sounds like it might work, but why do you keep saying "we"? Surely you won't be with us?'

Once again, Sandra tried to suppress her irritation at the implication behind this comment. She took a deep breath and replied, 'I am the leader here. I wouldn't ask of you anything that I would not do myself. Please don't think that just because I am a woman, I would expect to be left out of this very important operation. It is my plan. It is my responsibility.'

Michel looked at the other Maquis during the silence that ensued following Sandra's last remark. He knew some of those present would not expect a woman to take part in such a plan – let alone lead it. He decided to step in and said, 'Now listen. Sandra is an exceptional agent. She has already blown up the tunnel at Sainte-Catherine with the help of another woman agent. I know because I saw them do it! You have nothing to fear. We are fortunate to have her to lead us. Have faith in her. I do.'

Michel's words had the desired effect. Louis calmed down and sat down on the hay bale. He had been standing while directing his questions at Sandra. Alphonse stayed silent, appearing to suppress his own question. Charles and Henri maintained their silence. They knew just how determined Sandra could be from their previous meeting with her, and they knew of her success with Nancy in destroying the railway tunnel.

'Thank you, Michel,' said Sandra. 'Can we now get on with the detail of exactly how the destruction of this factory is to be achieved?'

'Of course,' was the unanimous response.

It took another twenty minutes of discussion to finalise the plan. Sandra, Alphonse, Charles and Henri would gain access to the site dressed as workers and then immediately access the explosives, which would have been delivered by truck previously, hidden in a consignment of component parts. They would then take the explosives to three separate locations within the factory: the boiler house, the machine shop and the main offices. All charges would be primed to go off at the same time, then they would leave the factory and join Michel and Louis, who would be waiting some distance away. All five would head for the woods, but then separate and go different ways to safety.

'Sounds a good plan. When do we carry it out?' asked Alphonse.

It was then that Sandra surprised everyone.

'The sooner the better. We are going to do it tonight. I have the workers' outfits ready for us here and the explosives are already on site. I arranged for their delivery this morning. We leave here now, so we can be in time to join the start of the 6pm shift and carry out our plan.'

'Now? Tonight? That was not what we expected!' Alphonse was obviously very surprised.

'Yes. Tonight. There is no time to waste.' Sandra turned towards a large box on the floor next to her as she spoke, opened it and handed Alphonse, Henri and Charles the workers' outfits.

'Please put these on, and then we will leave for the factory.'

Alphonse seemed disturbed by the suddenness of the operation as he said, 'Surely we should wait at least a day in order to warn those workers in the factory of our plan. Some of them may be killed as a result of what we intend to do.'

'We cannot do that,' said Sandra. 'To wait a day would increase the chances of someone finding out what we intend and could compromise the whole operation. We must act now.'

Alphonse shrugged his shoulders and, along with the others,

proceeded to put on the workers' overalls, which were all the same colour of green.

When they were all dressed, Sandra looked around and said, 'Right. We all know what we have to do. Let's do it!' With that remark the group set off for the factory on their bikes.

Sandra was a little put out by Alphonse's remarks. She knew that warning anyone in the factory of their plan would almost certainly lead to failure as the word would spread quickly, and many workers would have made sure they were not in the vicinity of the explosions. The plan may even have got to the Germans running the factory. Why had Alphonse questioned something so obvious?

Michel and Louis positioned themselves in what they knew was a safe house some distance from the factory. They bade farewell to Sandra and the others, and got themselves ready to provide covering fire if needed. They expected the others to return within the hour.

The area around the factory was quite busy as it was the shift changeover. There was much coming and going outside the factory gates. With all the activity, Sandra and the others managed to gain entry unnoticed. Surprisingly, they were not even searched. All four went straight to the storehouse where the recently arrived engine components were kept and each managed to obtain their respective load, which was wrapped in cloth, disguising its true contents. They each had their own targets, which they proceeded to visit alone. Timing was important. Sandra had planned that once the explosives were positioned, they would all set their fuses at the same time and then escape.

Sandra took her package to the main offices of the factory

where she left it under the stairs. She then waited a few minutes until the precise time, primed the detonator and walked towards the main entrance gates, where she was shortly joined by the three Maquis. At the gates an armed guard challenged them.

'*Où allez-vous?*' ('Where are you going?')

He spoke with a raised voice.

Sandra replied, '*Notre contremaître nous a demandé d'acheter de l'huile de garage dans la rue. Nous sommes à court.*' ('Our foreman has asked us to buy some oil from the garage down the street. We have run out.')

The guard waved them through the gates. Once outside, they quickly made their way towards the safe house where Michel and Louis were hiding. There they removed their overalls and waited for the explosions to come. They did not have long to wait.

The explosions all came within a few seconds of each other and were quickly followed by pandemonium in the streets as workers fled the factory. The resultant fires, particularly in the main offices of the factory, caused further disruption. Eventually a fire engine appeared.

'I think we can count this plan a success, don't you think?' Sandra addressed her remark to all in the room and it was met with a general rumble of approval. 'We will stay here a little longer, then leave individually and return to our respective safe places. Well done, everyone.'

Sandra and Michel were the last to leave the house. By then it was approaching 9pm and the roads around the factory were hectic. They managed to walk unnoticed through the streets. Almost everyone was too busy dealing with the mayhem caused by the explosions and the fire. It was beginning to get dark, but there was still enough light to help them find their bikes where they had left them and begin cycling back towards the farmhouse. Michel led the way.

'Not too fast, please!' Sandra shouted after him. He was some twenty yards in front and she did not want to lose sight of him, as she was not exactly sure of the way back to the farmhouse. Michel slowed down until they were cycling side by side. They were now some distance from the factory, but when Sandra turned round to look over her shoulder she could still see the flames caused by the explosions.

Michel and Sandra reached the farmhouse before midnight, went straight to their places of rest and fell asleep. There was no celebrating. As she dropped off to sleep, Sandra thought that if Nancy Lake had still been with them, she would have found a bottle of Calvados and toasted the successful outcome of their plan.

The next morning, Sandra and Michel shared breakfast with Claudette. It was not very often that the farmer's wife had time to eat with them so late in the morning. It was gone 9am when they started their meal.

'Patrice and I have a very busy day today. We are expecting delivery of some cows from a nearby farm. We purchased them last week in order to get our herd up to a suitable number. What are you two doing today?'

The calmness of Claudette's remarks was so delightful that one could almost imagine there was no war on at all.

'We will be contacting some friends nearby,' was all Michel would say. And indeed that was enough, considering what they had done the day before and the nature of their activities.

'This breakfast is lovely. Thank you so much,' said Sandra as she devoured the fried eggs with bacon, tomatoes and mushrooms. She almost thought it was worth staying in France and fighting the Nazis just for the breakfasts!

Claudette left them to finish while she went off to help Patrice prepare for the new arrivals. Sandra was washing up when there was a knock at the front door. Michel went to answer it. It was Charles. He came into the kitchen and sat at the table.

'What news?' asked Sandra.

'The factory is in ruins. The main offices were all destroyed by the fire and most of the machine tools have been severely damaged. It will take some time to repair everything and get back to anything like the level of production before our attack.'

'That's good. We did a thorough job,' said Michel.

'Yes,' agreed Charles, 'except for one thing.'

'What do you mean?' asked Sandra.

'The boiler house is still operational. The explosives did not go off there. It survived intact.'

'Must have been a faulty detonator,' remarked Michel.

Sandra made no comment. The boiler house was where Alphonse had been allocated. It was his job to plant the explosives there and blow it up. She had seen him carry the explosives towards the target and assumed all would be well, but she was beginning to have doubts about him. His failure to blow up the factory boiler house coupled with his comments about warning the employees was making her think something was not at all right with Alphonse.

Chapter 4

'Bobby Coles? Captured by the Gestapo? But how? Are you sure? He was such a brilliant agent and a dear friend. Please tell me there's been some mistake. Please!'

Sandra was very distressed by the news she had just been told. She had first met Bobby at the SOE training centre in Scotland and they had become friends. She knew he was operating with the Maquis in this region of France. Indeed, some of the Maquis who had worked with her had also worked with Bobby. She had never mentioned him by name, but she knew that they knew of him.

Michel looked resigned and said, 'No. Sorry. No mistake. He was arrested at Rouen station trying to board the train to Lisieux. The Germans knew what he was doing. We think there must have been an informant involved because his movements were kept secret – hardly anyone knew he was in France, let alone his exact whereabouts. It's a mystery how the Germans knew he was there.'

Sandra asked, 'Where is he being kept? We must try and rescue him. The Gestapo will kill him for sure. We must save him. We must!'

'That's impossible. He would have been taken to Rouen Tower for interrogation. No agent has ever come out of there alive. It's escape-proof. Its defences are beyond compare. I know because I used to work there before the war.'

Michel's tone sounded very defeatist to Sandra, which made her all the more determined to rescue Bobby. She thought for a moment, then sat down to weigh up all the options racing through her mind. How could she secure Bobby's escape? Michel said Rouen Tower was escape-proof, but there must be some way to overcome that. She would have to give this plenty of thought. Secondly, and probably more importantly, there must be an informer in the ranks, but who could it be? This question she must address – and quickly. If not, the whole of her operation in France would be compromised and could cause the deaths of many agents.

Sandra looked at Michel and asked, 'Who knew, or could possibly know, where Bobby was going and what he was doing?'

'Very few. Only myself, Henri, Charles and Alphonse. All are good agents – I have known them since the early days of the war. I cannot imagine that any one of them would inform the Gestapo about Bobby. But I think it would be a good idea to interview them all and try to discover if they let anyone else know what was going on.'

'A good idea,' agreed Sandra. 'However, let's not get them together all at the same time. Ask Charles and Henri to meet us somewhere other than here. Let's say on the edge of the forest near the farm, as soon as possible. We can involve Alphonse later.'

'OK. I will arrange for us to meet later tonight, say around 9pm at the crossroads on the edge of the forest. We can then walk to the farmhouse and have a talk in the adjacent barn. Leave it to me.'

'Yes. OK,' said Sandra. She was a little surprised that Michel had not asked why she was leaving Alphonse out of the planned meeting. She had her own reasons for doing it. A plan was taking shape in her mind regarding who might be informing the Gestapo about their operations and how to catch the culprit.

That evening, Sandra and Michel waited together at the crossroads. The spot was deserted. There was no traffic and it was almost dark. Charles and Henri arrived a little later than planned, which was not a surprise as they had to walk a long way from the village where they both lived. Having satisfied herself they were unaccompanied, Sandra called them over to where she and Michel were hiding.

'Glad you could both make it,' she said.

Henri acknowledged the greeting and asked, 'Why are we meeting here? Is it important?'

'Yes, very,' said Michel, 'but first follow me. We all need to sit down and discuss things.'

Slowly, the four of them tentatively made their way through the forest towards the farmhouse, about half a mile away. Michel knew the way, which was good, because otherwise they would have been stumbling around until daylight. Eventually, they reached the farmhouse where a light emanated from a front window. Bypassing it, they made their way into the barn where they were protected from the elements, and Michel lit a small lamp so they could at least see each other's faces.

'Well, what's this all about?' asked Charles.

Sandra looked at him and Henri and said, 'We have reason to believe there is an informer in our organisation, and we need your help in finding out who it is. Bobby Coles, an SOE agent, has been arrested by the Gestapo and is being held in Rouen Tower. He was betrayed. The Gestapo arrested him at Rouen railway station. They knew who he was and where he was going. That information must have been fed to them by an informer. We have to find out who is behind this and stop them.'

'You're right. Have you any ideas who the informant might be?' asked Charles.

'Not yet, but we are working on it. Any thoughts or ideas you might have, please share with us. But first we need a plan to help Bobby escape. He is important to us and we must try to save him from what will be almost certain death at the hands of the Gestapo. Any ideas?'

Michel was amused and impressed by Sandra's approach. She was turning what he thought would be an interrogation into a joint effort to plan an escape. She was testing both agents to see if they were prepared to carry out what he considered an impossible operation.

'Rouen Tower is said to be impregnable,' commented Henri, 'though I think we might be able to find a way of getting in and rescuing Bobby. I have an idea that could work.'

'Let's know what it is,' urged Sandra.

The four heads moved closer towards one another.

'First, we must set up a diversion – some kind of activity in the forest, visible from the tower – that will bring some of the German troops out to investigate. Second, two of us will gain entry to the castle through the underground sewer – and, yes, I know it's securely protected, but we will cut through the iron barriers there prior to mounting our operation. Once inside, Michel, who knows the layout of the interior, will be able to lead us to where Bobby is most likely being interrogated. We will have to overpower the guards there and take Bobby with us out of the castle. Lastly, while we are in the castle, the German troops will have discovered our diversion in the forest and we will set up a second diversion, and perhaps even a third, that will keep them occupied while we escape with Bobby. I suggest the second diversion be some form of explosion against the castle walls on the opposite side from the sewer entrance. It should provide enough of a distraction to the Germans for us to make good our escape with the minimum of opposition. What do you think?'

The three of them sat in silence for a short while. The plan sounded reasonable. How did he think of it so quickly? Michel looked up and mused, 'As you say, no agent has ever managed to get free from Rouen Tower. But I like your plan, so let's do it!'

This was enough for Sandra. What was going to be an interrogation had been turned into something far more positive, and all four of them were in agreement. She prayed it would work.

'What about Alphonse? Will he be with us?' said Charles.

'No. He is doing something else,' replied Sandra, who quickly continued, 'No one else must know about this, and we must act as quickly as possible. I suggest tomorrow night. Michel and I will break into the castle while you both set up the diversions. Is that agreed?'

Henri and Charles looked a little surprised, and Charles commented, 'Well, yes, but would it not be better if one of us took your place inside the castle? After all, you are only a woman. We would be better at dealing with the troops, don't you think?'

Sandra managed to control her anger at Charles' remark, merely looking daggers at him, and saying, 'Bugger off! Michel and I will gain entry and rescue Bobby. And later this week you will treat me to an evening out and repent your thoughtless remarks.'

Michel looked worried and said, 'Charles, you must accept that Sandra is leading us. She is in charge and I know she is an exceptional operative. Please be kinder with your remarks!'

Silence ensued until Charles apologised for what he had said, after which Sandra continued, 'Right. We will meet here tomorrow evening at 7pm. Make sure all the necessary gear is ready and available. We will finalise the details then. OK?'

'Yes, of course,' was the joint response.

The following evening at 7pm the four met at the barn. They were all laden with lots of additional equipment, including explosives. Charles was the first to speak.

'I will lay this explosive at the base of the castle wall. It probably won't breach the wall, but it will cause quite a distraction. I will detonate it as soon as I see the German troops reach our first diversion, which Henri will now tell you about.'

Henri pulled from his haversack what looked like a torch attached to a rope.

'This will be attached to a tree on the opposite side of the castle from Charles' explosives. As soon as you signal to me with your torch that you can get through the sewer barrier, I will switch it on and fire my gun to attract the Germans' attention. I will then join Charles where we can see what's going on and wait. We will hope that both you and Bobby manage to get out of the castle by the time the troops have reacted to the explosion. Then, if necessary, we'll provide covering fire to enable your escape.'

Sandra looked impressed and said, 'Great. Michel and I will go down to the sewer entrance and begin cutting through the barrier. As you say, we will signal to you as soon as we can gain access through it. Good luck, everyone. Let's go.'

Sandra and Michel spent a good half hour slowly sawing through the iron bars at the sewer entrance. They were as quiet as possible, not wishing to attract any attention from the German garrison. Even so, every rasp made by the saw sounded loud to their ears. Eventually, they managed to make an opening large enough to get through, at which point they signalled to Henri to begin the distraction. They then squeezed through the opening and, bent double, made their way along the sewer tunnel.

Upon receiving the signal, Henri fired his gun into the air and switched on the torch, which he had tied to an upper branch of a tree, and set it in motion. He hoped the wind would keep it swinging. He then made his way to the other side of the woods, near where Charles was ready to begin the second distraction by exploding the charge set in the castle wall. All was going well so far.

The light from the torch was soon spotted by a German sentry, who raised the alarm. A number of troops were sent from the castle towards the light. All had their rifles at the ready as they approached it. Activity in and around the castle was becoming more animated.

After just a few dozen yards, Sandra and Michel reached a grating in the roof of the tunnel. They could hear no noise from above, so they pushed the grating out and climbed up into what seemed like some kind of storeroom. They waited quietly for a few moments to make sure there was no one around.

Michel whispered, 'We are in one of the ground-floor storerooms. I remember it from when I worked here. Let's go along the corridor and see if we can locate where they are keeping Bobby. Follow me.'

Slowly, Michel opened the storeroom door and looked along the corridor. He could see no one. Entering the corridor, they made their way quietly along, hoping to find the room where Bobby would be subject to interrogation. They did not have to look far. At the end of the corridor, a door was partly open and a light was on inside. They crept slowly up to the door and gently pushed it open. Inside, tied to a chair and with his face and clothes covered in blood, sat Bobby. He didn't even bother to look up when they entered, assuming it would be more torture from the Gestapo.

Sandra produced a knife and, while cutting the ropes that secured him to the chair, remarked, 'Well, you can at least look pleased to see us. Come on!'

Bobby suddenly raised his head. What's going on? This can't be for real! he thought.

Sandra had cut all the ropes. 'Come on, now! We have to get you out of here quickly! Stand up.'

Bobby tried to stand, but his legs gave way. He had been tied to the chair for more than two days, not even allowed to use the toilet. Consequently, his legs were numb and stiff. He was not only covered in blood around his face and neck from the beatings he had endured, but also in urine and faeces around his trousers. He looked an absolute mess.

Sandra and Michel held Bobby and almost dragged him towards the door. At last he managed to get some words out.

'Who are you?'

Sandra was not surprised Bobby did not recognise her. He was in quite a state. She replied, 'We'll tell you later, but we're here to help. Just concentrate on staying upright.'

Michel suddenly stopped walking as they all heard the sound of boots coming along the corridor. They bundled Bobby behind the door as the handle turned and it began to open. Sandra had already pulled her gun from its holster and was aiming it at the door.

At that moment, there came a loud explosion from nearby. It must be the second diversionary tactic, they thought. From the other side of the door came the sound of running as whoever was about to enter changed their mind and made off towards the explosion.

'Let's go!' Michel hissed as he and Sandra hustled Bobby along the corridor towards the storeroom. They reached it in seconds and entered. Michel shoved some boxes behind the closed door to slow down anyone who might try to follow them.

'Now, Bobby, we have to lower you into the sewer drain. Are you ready?'

A nod and a mumbled 'Yes' was all Bobby could manage as he was slowly lowered through the hole. He tried to stand on the wet floor, but found it too difficult so just leaned against the wall as Sandra and Michel followed him down. Michel replaced the grating and the three of them started along the passage towards the entrance. This was slow, because Bobby was so weak and there was very little room to help him. Eventually they reached the entrance to the sewer where they had removed the iron bars. There was a lot of noise outside. The Germans had been galvanised into action by the explosion and were everywhere to be seen, running around with their guns at the ready. Sandra, Michel and Bobby stopped where they were and waited until they were sure they would not be seen running across the open ground and into the forest. At least, they would try to run, but it seemed that might not be possible for Bobby.

'Do you think you can make it?' asked Michel, looking at Bobby.

'I'll try my best, but I may need someone to help me just a little.'

Together, after satisfying themselves no Germans were in sight, they made a dash for the woods.

Bobby tried his best, but he was in difficulties from the start. Halfway across the open ground, he had to stop, so Michel and Sandra each took an arm and helped him hobble into the woods. They made it to the cover of the trees just in time as two German soldiers came around the corner of the tower.

'Get down! Lie still,' Sandra said quietly. The two Germans were looking in their direction. Sandra and Michel both got out their pistols and waited, hoping the two German soldiers would leave them alone. However, they seemed to be getting ready to approach where the three of them were hiding. Their rifles were pointing towards them and Sandra feared the worst. Both she and Michel raised and aimed their pistols at the two Germans.

'*Beachtung! Komm her. Wir haben mehr Sprengstoffe gefunden!*' ('Attention! Come over here. We have found more explosives!')

The voice came from their right. It was a German officer

giving orders, which were obeyed instantly by the two soldiers, who ran towards him.

What a relief! They were now free to move from where they were hiding. Michel got to his feet and helped Bobby up.

'Come on. Let's get as far from here as we can!'

Sandra led the way through the woods. She could hear the commotion and babble of German voices taking place behind them and could only imagine what Charles and Henri had provided in the way of distractions. Whatever they had done, it had worked!

As they approached the other side of the woods, Bobby became slower and slower, struggling with the effects of his injuries. Sandra and Michel were almost carrying him forward. They had arranged to hide for the night near the safe house, but not in it nor in the barn, because it was almost a certainty that the surrounding area would be searched when Bobby's escape was discovered. A small underground room, created by the Maquis, had been prepared for them. When they reached it, Michel opened the hatch and together they dragged Bobby inside. They tucked him up in the sleeping bag there trying to make him comfortable. Sandra gave him water to drink and some biscuits to eat. There was nothing they could do about the appalling stink. A good wash and some fresh clothes would have to wait until it was safe.

The three of them stayed in the small hideaway through the night. Bobby managed to sleep for the first time since his capture by the Gestapo, who had never allowed him the luxury of sleep for any length of time. Michel and Sandra only managed to doze. They were both very much aware of the situation they were in and alert to any sounds outside.

When dawn broke, Michel came out of their underground refuge and carefully looked all around. He could see no one.

'Looks like we could make our way back to the farmhouse.'

Michel turned around and saw that Sandra had come out of the refuge right behind him.

'Yes, and I think we could wake up Bobby now and check he's OK.'

Michel nodded agreement.

They returned to the hideaway where Bobby was still sleeping. They gently woke him and offered him some water, which he took gratefully.

'Thank you, both! Thank you! But how did you manage to get me out of that hellhole? I thought it was all over for me. The Germans knew where I was and had an idea of what I was planning to do. I told them nothing. I'm so glad to be alive. I owe you both so much. How did you do it?'

Bobby was becoming more animated, already so different from how he was when they had rescued him. This was encouraging.

'Well, it wasn't easy, but we will tell you all about it when we get to our safe house. First, we have to leave here and make our way undetected. The Germans are likely to be everywhere, so we must be very careful.' Sandra was helping Bobby to his feet as she said this.

When he had stood up, he said, 'Of course. I'm feeling a bit stronger. Just point me in the right direction and let's go.'

The three of them made their way towards the farmhouse, stopping every few minutes to listen and make sure they were not being watched or followed. They made it to the barn after about thirty minutes. Bobby was still a little slow in his movements, but both Michel and Sandra could tell he was getting stronger all the time.

In the barn a meal of bread, eggs and bacon for each of them was savoured, together with plenty of water to drink – this after Bobby had been directed to the wash house for a strip wash in cold water and given some old clothes to wear, which Claudette had found for him. Bobby was so thankful to get rid of the stink that surrounded him.

'Sandra, it's great to see you again,' he said. 'I always knew you were going to be a top-notch agent. Thank you for rescuing me – and please tell me how you managed this incredible escape!'

Michel described how they achieved the outcome by means of diversionary tactics, with the help of Charles and Henri. It was quite a story, thought Michel, even as he told it.

'That's marvellous! Well done and thank you again. But I have to say that it does look as if there is someone, somewhere, who knows much of what's going on within our organisation and is letting the Germans know about it. I believe there is an informer somewhere.'

'I agree with you. We must find out who it is and deal with him as soon as possible,' said Sandra. After finishing the meal, Bobby was taken by Michel to another safe house some miles away to await rescue from London. It was important he should lie low for the time being.

The village of Bourg-Achard was very quiet. It was just after 6am, the day after the rescue and escape of Bobby Coles from Rouen Castle. The village was just a few miles from Rouen and was a very peaceful place despite the occupation of France by the Germans. It was a small farming village with little industry and had not attracted much attention from the occupying forces. Most of the villagers had managed to remain free from contact with the enemy and had got on with their lives. But the peace and quiet of Bourg-Achard was about to be shattered for ever.

The village was beginning to stir to face the busy day ahead when the sound of armoured trucks became louder and louder as a force of Nazi troops entered the square. The soldiers got out of their trucks and, under orders from their officers, began knocking on the doors of houses very loudly. As the doors were opened, the soldiers forcibly entered, soon coming out with any male occupants and marching them, at gunpoint, towards the armoured trucks. The villagers' hands were tied as they were roughly bundled aboard. Some of the men's wives and mothers followed them to the trucks, crying, screaming and demanding to know what was going on, but the Nazi troops ignored them.

Within ten minutes around thirty men had been forced into one of the trucks. The officer in charge called a halt to the door-knocking and recalled his men to the village square. What was happening? The women whose husbands and sons had been forcibly taken had congregated and were distraught, terrified about what was going to happen to their loved ones. Would they be taken away and imprisoned? But what had they done? Tragically, they were soon to find out.

The truck with the thirty captives started its engine and, closely followed by the armed soldiers, drove slowly to the outskirts of the village. There the German commandant ordered the men to be pulled from the truck and lined up along the bank of the river that flowed through the village towards the sea. The Germans had positioned machine guns there, pointing at the Frenchmen. At a shouted directive from the commandant, the soldiers opened fire on the completely defenceless village men, shooting them dead. As the men fell, they dropped into the river. There were loud screams from the men and horrified cries from the women, who had followed the truck and witnessed this appalling scene and the awful death of their loved ones.

When the shooting was finished, some of the troops were ordered towards the spot where the victims had stood to make sure those who had not already fallen into the river were pushed in. About five men had fallen but not reached their watery grave and were lying on the riverbank. The German troops just kicked them over the edge into the water. One village woman was screaming at the top of her voice as she tried to reach her dead husband. As he was pushed into the river she sank to her knees, sobbing and wailing.

The officer called all his men back. They loaded their machine guns into the trucks, which just drove away from the village, leaving behind scores of distraught and weeping women and children. What had they done to deserve this?

There was no possible way that anyone in the village could think straight for some time. This had been the most appalling mass murder. It was later that day, however, that it became apparent why the Germans had committed this crime. The villagers realised this heinous action was the Nazi retaliation for the escape of Bobby Coles.

Michel and Sandra were together in the barn adjacent to the safe house when Charles entered and gave them the news about the mass murder. They were both speechless and received the news with enormous misgivings. They felt they were partly to blame. Sandra determined to seek revenge. She resolved that she would do everything she could to destroy the Gestapo headquarters in Elbeuf and kill as many Nazis as she could at the same time – even if she had to do it all by herself. Michel was distraught. He had some relatives, an aunt and uncle, who lived in Bourg-Achard. He prayed that they were not victims. He decided to go to the village immediately to find out so, bidding Sandra farewell, he and Charles left the barn and headed for Bourg-Achard.

Sandra slumped in the corner of the barn. She felt terrible. What could she do to exact revenge? This was war – and in war anything goes. But this crime was beyond belief. To kill thirty innocent men in front of their families – what kind of people were these bloody Nazis?

Claudette had come into the barn with some coffee. She had been told what had happened at Bourg-Achard and tried to comfort Sandra. Sandra appreciated her kindness, but it acted as a trigger to release the pent-up emotions of the past few days and Claudette could only watch helplessly as Sandra wept uncontrollably.

Michel and Charles reached the village and found many people just sitting around outside, looking distraught and crying. There was little they could do to comfort the bereaved. Some of the villagers had tried to collect the bodies of loved ones from the river, but it was proving difficult because the river was quite deep at the place where the hostages were killed. They all felt completely helpless in the circumstances.

A priest was conspicuous in the village square. He was gathering small groups of people together and praying for them and their dead. Afterwards, he led folk off to the church to join the many other people congregating there to comfort one another and show their unity and resolve. Michel and Charles went with them. Then Michel spotted his aunt, who was sitting in a pew on her own, crying. He feared the worst.

'*Tatie Edith! C'est moi Michel*,' ('Aunty Edith! It is I, Michel,') he said as he put his arm around her. She looked up at him and sobbed.

She replied, '*Ils lui ont tire dessus. Ils ont abattu Pierre. Il est parti.*' ('They shot him. They shot Pierre dead. He is gone.')

Michel wrapped both arms around his aunt and tried to console her. They wept together. Similar scenes were being repeated all around the church as families, in a state of shock, tried to come to terms with their losses. It was a black day.

After a while, Michel and Charles left the church. Michel promised his aunt that he would return later that day to be with her as a comfort. Just as they were leaving by the main door of the church, a sound of joyful shouting came from a woman and her daughter, who was calling out 'Papa, Papa!' at the top of her voice.

What was going on?

When Michel and Charles got outside, they saw a man in soaking wet and dirty clothes, being hugged by his wife and child, and surrounded by a group of excited villagers. Charles waited for an appropriate moment and asked, '*Ce qui vous est arrive?*' ('What happened to you?')

The man looked up from holding his wife and replied, '*Je savais qu'ils nous tireraient tous dessus. J'ai juste attend que les armes se mettent en marche et j'ai plonge dans la riviere avant d'etre touche. C'etait un peu difficile d'essayer de nager avec les mains attachees derriere le dos, mais lorsque votre vie en depend, vous faites le necessaire.'* ('I knew they would shoot us all. I just waited for the guns to start and dived into the river before I was hit. It was a bit difficult trying to swim with my hands tied behind my back, but when your life depends upon it you do whatever is necessary.')

'Vous avez survecu!' ('You survived!')

'Oui. Dieu merci.' ('Yes. Thank God.')

The man continued to comfort his wife and child while other family members around him embraced each other. The reunited family eventually entered the sanctuary of the church, which had become a place of refuge for many.

Charles and Michel left to return to the barn. They would never forget what they had just witnessed. It would forever affect the way they felt towards the Nazis.

Chapter 5

'Have you heard the news? It's wonderful! The Allies have landed and are fighting their way through Normandy as I speak. The war will soon be over!'

'Steady there,' said Sandra. 'There is still a long way to go and much work to be done. We have to be prepared for whatever is asked of us. There is much we will be expected to do before peace rules again.'

'Yes, but even you must be overjoyed at the news! Hitler now has to fight on two fronts. He cannot last much longer.' Charles' enthusiasm was contagious to most around him, but it had no effect on Sandra.

She looked serious and said, 'Let's just temper our thoughts with some realism. We will be asked, I'm sure, to provide every possible support to our troops as they fight through France. I am waiting now for a message from London regarding what actions we need to take. Then we will meet and decide what is best to do.'

Charles nodded his approval.

Sandra continued, 'There is one thing we must do quickly. It will cause maximum disruption in our area and will undoubtedly help our troops as they advance.'

'What is that?' asked Michel, who, with Charles and Sandra, made up the threesome meeting to discuss the next stage of their plans. They were inside the barn. It would be very unlikely that Claudette or her husband, Patrice, in the farmhouse knew they were there.

'We must attack and destroy the Gestapo headquarters at Elbeuf as soon as possible. A surprise assault from two directions is my plan. We will need about ten Maquis and plenty of ammunition. If we can wipe out their headquarters and those inside it, we will strike a blow for the Allied advance and provide some retribution for the murder of the men at Bourg-Achard. Yes?'

'Yes,' said Michel enthusiastically. He could think of nothing but revenge. Nothing! He felt that all he wanted was to kill as many Nazis as possible, and the sooner the better. Looking at Sandra, he asked, 'And what exactly is your plan? We have never done anything like this before. You must know that the Gestapo headquarters are very well defended. We would have to be thoroughly prepared to succeed.'

Charles agreed with everything Michel said. They both knew this would be a dangerous operation, but they would do anything to exact revenge on those murderous Nazis for what they had done.

Sandra produced a small map from her rucksack and

spread it on the hay bale in front of them. It showed the Gestapo headquarters and surrounding streets in Elbeuf. Sandra pointed at the headquarters and said, 'There it is. There are the two streets we will use to approach it, so we can attack from opposite sides of the building. We will take no prisoners and destroy the building by burning it to the ground. We will not make a full-frontal assault – that would be too dangerous and costly. We must gain access quietly and kill quietly before blowing the place up. I would like this done tomorrow night. Are you both in agreement?'

Michel was the first to answer. 'It sounds feasible, but I would expect some losses. Are we prepared to risk that? And who is to lead the assault?'

'I will be leading it, of course. And, please, no comments regarding women putting themselves in danger! My job is to help our troops achieve freedom for the civilised world. Freedom is the only thing worth fighting for. It really doesn't matter if I die, because without freedom there is no point in living.'

Michel and Charles were silent. They had never heard anyone sum up what they did and why they did it in such a short but inspiring manner. There was no possible response other than to embrace Sandra and agree with everything she had said, which is what they both did.

On the morning of the planned assault on the Gestapo headquarters at Elbeuf, Sandra held a meeting with the Maquis to finalise the method of attack.

'Some of you will be familiar with the headquarters building. Before the Nazi occupation, it had been the local police station. It's a substantial building and also provides rooms for some German officers. There is a front and a rear entrance, and the building is guarded most of the time during the day. At night, most doors are locked.

'First, four of us will gain entry to the building with the minimum of fuss. I will lead you in this. Once I have gained entry safely, I will signal to the rest of you to follow. We must not arouse any suspicion or attract attention. Once inside, we will kill the occupants and plant our charges where they will do the most damage, as fast as possible. Those of you positioned outside the building will deal with any German soldiers who may be attracted to find out what is going on inside and, if necessary, provide covering fire to protect our escape. After the charges are planted, we will meet up and leave the building together, then run to our meeting point in the nearby woods. Once there, we can confirm the success of our activity and make good our escape to our safe houses. Any questions?'

Sandra's outline plan was well received, but there were a few questions. The first came from Henri. 'Who will be going inside and who will be staying outside?'

'There will be four of us going into the building: Michel, Charles, Rupert and I. Rupert is key to this, because he was a policeman based in the building before the occupation and he knows the layout very well. He will know the best places to plant our explosives. The other four – Henri, Richard, Anton and William – will remain outside, suitably positioned to provide covering fire if needed when we leave. The charges will be set on a short fuse – less than two minutes – so no hanging about!'

'What about any prisoners in the cells? There are sure to be some there. We cannot let them be blown to pieces. Will we not help them escape?' The questioner was Anton. He had joined the Maquis at the start of the war and helped Michel a number of times in different Resistance operations.

'That's a good question. Rupert will check out the cells as a priority and try to release any prisoners there. We believe there may be at least two Canadian POWs, who escaped from their prison camp in Germany some time ago, but were recaptured recently on a train heading to Marseille. Once they are released, Rupert will signal to us and the charges will be primed.'

Richard asked, 'What if the Germans decide to take revenge for our actions and select another village where they kill dozens of innocent people, including women and children?'

Sandra held back as Michel answered, 'If we let that possibility stop us, we will never win this war.'

Sandra added, 'We cannot allow that to stop us. This is war. We are fighting an enemy the like of which has never been seen before. Without our determination to succeed, no matter what the cost, France and the rest of the free world will be in chains. I know this is difficult. What happened at Bourg-Achard was heinous, but we must fight on. Fight on and win. We must free France.'

Richard nodded approval. They all knew what Sandra said was true, but they also knew the possibility of German retaliation was likely.

'Any more questions?' asked Michel.

'Yes. What explosives have we got?' This came from William. He was probably one of the experts on explosives in the group, having taken part in a few operations with Michel to blow up railway lines. 'Will they be good enough to destroy the headquarters?'

'The explosives we will be using are the latest to be air-dropped from London. We will each carry thirty pounds in our backpacks, which should be enough to destroy at least the interior of the building. Once in place, we will set the fuses for two minutes and make a dash for the forest.'

The group murmured their agreement.

Michel then encouraged the group to disband. Being together too long increased the risk of being discovered by the Germans. They would next meet up immediately prior to their raid on the Gestapo headquarters. They were to meet in a nearby safe house when it was dark and from there launch their attack.

Sandra checked her watch. It was 10.30pm and dark outside. The team were all assembled in the safe house just a few hundred yards from the Gestapo headquarters. She decided to make a move.

'Bonne chance à tous.' ('Good luck, everyone.')

With that comment, Sandra led the team out the front door into the street. Each man knew exactly what he had to do. Henri, Richard, Anton and William positioned themselves near the exits from the headquarters. They made sure they were well hidden. Meanwhile, Michel, Charles, Rupert and Sandra made their way towards the entrance at the side of the building. They could see that it was not guarded – at least not on the outside, though it would almost certainly have a sentry positioned immediately inside the door. Sandra had a plan to deal with the sentry, which is why she had decided to dress in what could only be described as a provocative manner and was wearing plenty of make-up.

Sandra slowly approached the entrance and began to put on a friendly manner. The other three members of the team held back while she entered the building.

'*Bleib wo du bist!*' ('Stay where you are!')

The order was shouted at her in German and, as she looked in the direction it came from, she could see the rifle pointing straight at her head.

'*Wer bist du?*' ('Who are you?')

The soldier was very insistent and demanded a quick answer.

'*Oh, monsieur, je me suis égaré. Pouvez-vous me dire comment aller au café Salut? Je rencontre mon ami là-bas.*' ('Oh, sir, I have lost my way. Can you tell me how to get to the café Salut? I am meeting my friend there.')

Sandra answered in French, fluttered her eyelashes and smiled at the soldier. She looked a veritable treat with her make-up and attractive outfit.

'*Du solltest nicht hier sein. Dies ist das Hauptquartier der Gestapo. Du must jetzt gehen.*' ('You should not be here. This is the Gestapo headquarters. You must leave now.')

Again, the soldier was insistent, but at least he had lowered his rifle, which was now pointing towards the ground. Sandra continued smiling and answered in a very soft and alluring manner.

'*Oh, merci mon ami. Je vais devoir aller chercher le café Salut par moi-même.*' ('Oh, thank you, my friend. I will have to try to find the café Salut on my own.')

As Sandra said this, she moved slightly closer to the soldier, who appeared a little more relaxed – caused, no doubt, by the attractive young lady in front of him. Though he could hardly understand a word of French, it made no difference. As he was pointing towards the exit he could only see a lovely woman who now gripped his attention. If only I had time to make something of this, he thought.

Sandra came even closer to the soldier. She knew that he had now dropped his guard. Indeed, his rifle was just dangling from one hand, while the other seemed to want to touch her, if only to direct her towards the exit. Sandra reached inside the front of her dress and gripped her pistol. Now was the time to act.

Quickly she produced the pistol, pointed it at the soldier's chest and pulled the trigger twice. The noise from the pistol was quite subdued as she had wrapped the barrel in cloth to help silence it. The soldier fell in a heap before her. She grabbed his rifle and made for the door, where she signalled to the others to enter.

Michel, Charles and Rupert entered quietly and helped Sandra push the dead soldier away from the door. They were all now ready to do what they had come to do. They climbed the stairs that led from the entrance to the first floor. The whole building was silent. Michel knew the main communications room and sleeping quarters were on the first floor. They approached the door to the sleeping quarters and each produced a grenade, which they activated and threw into the room. They dived for cover away from the door.

The explosions were loud and accompanied by the cries of some in the sleeping quarters. The team showed no mercy. As the Gestapo officers pushed themselves through the door, away from the carnage inside, they were met by a hail of fire from Sandra and the others. All were cut down. The gunfire and explosions attracted soldiers from the floor above, who came running downstairs to see what was going on. Again, Sandra and the team showed no mercy. They shot each German as he came down the stairs. There were no survivors.

After a few moments, all the noise stopped. Sandra and

Michel looked at one another. Michel said, 'Quick! Let's plant the explosives now.'

Sandra, Michel and Charles started planting their own explosives in various positions around the now bloody building. As they did, Rupert came running up the stairs, having been down to the cells to search for prisoners.

'The cells were all empty. No prisoners here,' said Rupert.

'Great!' Michel shouted. 'Now set the fuses for two minutes on my command.'

Michel waited in silence for some ten seconds. He was hoping to hear nothing from outside. He did not want to leave the building and meet a group of Nazis. He couldn't hear anything.

'Right. Set the fuses NOW!'

Within seconds they had done so, and the four of them ran down the stairs, through the door and out into the street. They took cover behind a garden wall. Lights were coming on in the houses around, which was understandable given the commotion caused by the gunfire. The explosion was tremendous when it came. Bits of brick and building parts were showered all around. Some pieces broke the windows of houses in the vicinity. Michel looked up first from behind the garden wall. He could see amid all the smoke and fire that they had been successful. The building looked an absolute mess. He turned to the others lying around him.

'Come on, let's head towards the woods.'

Together they ran down the street towards the woods and safety. As they ran, the houses all around were stirring as lights were turned on and people came into the street to see for themselves what had happened. They quickly got to the end of the street and turned towards the woods, which were just a few hundred yards away.

The noise behind them increased as more and more people came out to see what was going on, and they heard the sound of motor engines, which could only mean that German soldiers had entered the area. Rupert momentarily stopped and turned around to see what was behind them. He did not like what he saw. Along the street he could see some soldiers looking in their direction with raised rifles. They must have been nearby when the explosions had gone off. The soldiers began shooting at them.

'Look out! They are firing at us!' he shouted.

Those were his last words. A bullet hit his chest and he fell to the ground.

Michel shouted, 'Leave him! Leave him! We must get away. Run!'

The three of them managed to get into the woods without further loss. They turned around and began firing back at the Germans, using the trees as cover. The German soldiers did not stop. They came running into the woods, shooting in front of them at random. The soldiers were now easy targets for Sandra, Michel and Charles, as the light coming from the village showed them up. They were shot down soon after entering the woods.

'Follow me,' called Sandra as soon as she saw the last soldier fall. There was no point in staying where they were. More soldiers would follow, and they would eventually be so outnumbered they would all be shot. They had to escape and get as much distance as possible between themselves and the Nazi soldiers.

They scrambled through the forest as fast as possible. Every so often, they would stop and listen, but not for long. It was far too dangerous to wait. They knew there would soon be dozens, or even hundreds, of soldiers scouring the woods for them. After the destruction of their headquarters, the Gestapo would stop at nothing to catch the culprits.

Sandra wondered what happened to the other four members of the Resistance team, who had guarded the entrance while they went inside. There had been no sign of Henri, Richard, Anton or William when they left the headquarters and took cover from the explosion. Since then, there had been little time to think of anything beyond their own safety and escape. She hoped they had got away.

The woods seemed to be getting more and more difficult to get through as they moved forward. However, Michel knew them well and was leading them through at a pretty fast pace.

'Keep going. We will soon be clear,' he said.

After about thirty minutes of scrabbling through the densely wooded area of forest, during which they must have covered about two miles, Michel said, 'Stop here. Let's see what's around.'

Sandra and Charles were glad of the respite, however temporary. The three of them sat still on the grass next to a tree, and whispered to each other.

'Rupert was a good Maquis. One of the best.' Charles was very obviously upset to lose his friend.

'So true. A good man. We will honour his name.' Michel's reply told Sandra exactly how these very brave men were regarded by their compatriots. What a team they made.

'A courageous man,' she agreed.

They all sat quietly for a few moments as they took stock of the position they were in.

'What shall we do now? Shall we wait until morning or continue on towards greater safety?' Charles questioned.

'We must keep going as far as possible in the dark. I would expect many German soldiers to be scouring the whole area when daylight comes. The further away we are the better. If we can reach the barn at the farmhouse by daybreak, we will be safe. If we take the right path, we can make it.' Michel sounded confident.

'Agreed,' said Sandra, 'but what about the others? We have not seen them since we blew up the headquarters.'

'We cannot afford to wait for them. They could be anywhere. We must get going.' What Michel said made sense. They really could not spend their time looking for the other members of their team. Escape to safety was the priority.

Michel continued to lead the other two through the woods. He had a good idea that it would take another three hours of walking to get to the barn. By then, it would be around 6am and it would be light. They kept moving without any further stops until they reached the edge of the woods. Michel told them they would have to cross about four fields of open countryside before they reached the woods near where the barn and farmhouse were. He surveyed the fields in front of them and, seeing nothing untoward, led them across, keeping close to the boundary hedges, until they reached the woods on the other side. They had made good progress.

'How much further?' asked Sandra.

'About another thirty minutes,' replied Michel.

They were almost home.

The barn was before them, and Sandra, Michel and Charles entered through the secret door at the rear. They made no sound and hid themselves among the hay bales. They had determined to remain as quiet as possible for as long as they could. The expectation that German soldiers would be searching the area was on their minds and they did not want to give themselves away. There was a small store of food and water where they were hiding, and they availed themselves of it. Their conversation was whispered. Michel spoke first.

'Well done, both of you. We have struck back at the Gestapo and they will take some time to recover from what we have done. Well done.'

Sandra agreed and sought to reassure them both by saying they should be safe where they were, but they would need to remain here for at least another day before they could contemplate further operations. They agreed they would let Claudette know they were in the barn later that day and get her to supply them with more food and drink. Charles agreed, though he looked disconsolate despite their survival. The death of Rupert had affected him deeply.

As the morning wore on, Sandra found herself falling into sleep and then waking with a start as the sound of farm animals or Michel and Charles talking disturbed her. It was not surprising she felt tired. She had hardly slept for the best part of two days.

It was about midday when the sound of the secret door at the rear of the barn being opened concentrated their minds and made all three reach for their pistols. They stayed silent and pointed their weapons towards the noise, waiting.

A shape emerged from the entrance and they tightened their grip on their weapons, but then, thankfully, relaxed it. It was Henri.

'Thank God!' cried Michel. 'You are safe.'

As Henri looked towards them, he returned the welcome with a shout of joy.

'You're here! We were so worried that you had all been shot.'

'Likewise,' said Charles.

It was then that the others came through the secret entrance, but only two more. Standing before them were Henri, Richard and Anton. They all looked much relieved to be with them in the comparative safety of the barn.

'Where is William?' asked Sandra. 'What happened?'

'He died protecting our escape. After the second explosion, there were so many soldiers outside the headquarters that we were spotted and they opened fire on us. We decided to make a break into the woods and William provided us with covering fire. We ran while he just kept shooting at the German soldiers. We guess that eventually he ran out of ammunition and they shot him. He would have been outnumbered twenty to one. Such a brave Maquis.' Anton choked on the last words.

'And where is Rupert?' asked Henri.

Michel and Sandra told the others what had happened to them and how Rupert had met his fate. They had started as eight and now they were six.

Henri spoke first after a few seconds of silence.

'We have been hiding in the forest since our escape. We did not want to try to find our way here in the dark. We were fortunate in that, although on a couple of occasions German soldiers came near to where we were hiding, we escaped detection. Can we say that our operation was a success?'

'Most certainly,' said Michel. 'We have dealt them a blow from which they will take a long time to recover – if at all. The Allies are advancing ever forward through Normandy and we pray they will be here soon. We have done well.'

A murmur of satisfaction greeted Michel's remarks, though obviously tempered by the loss of their two friends, William and Rupert.

Sandra spoke next. 'As we agreed earlier, I think it might be a good idea to let Claudette know we are here. She will be able to get some more food and water for us. We must all stay here until tomorrow morning and then leave at different times to minimise the possibility of capture. Agreed?'

There was no dissent. Michel left the barn to let Claudette know they were there and get more food. He was gone for about five minutes. When he returned, he told them that Claudette would be bringing some food for them soon.

As he reflected on the activities of the past few days, Michel realised how glad he was that his group of Maquis were being led by Sandra.

Chapter 6

The successful escape of Bobby Coles from Rouen Castle, with the help of Michel, Charles and Henri, had helped to focus Sandra's mind. She now had little doubt that there was an informer in the organisation. The ambush and arrest of Bobby showed quite clearly that the Gestapo knew what he had planned. Who could it be? Sandra had her own idea, but who could she discuss it with? Who could she trust? Her mind was a turmoil of thought. The informer must be dealt with quickly or the whole of her operation, and many Allied lives, would be at risk. Nazi lines of communication and supply must be destroyed. The operations of the Wehrmacht must be disrupted.

Of course, she guessed that there was really only one culprit. There were five people who knew that Coles was going to be at the railway station at the time he was arrested. They were herself, Michel, Henri, Charles and Alphonse. Following the escape, she knew she could trust Michel, Charles and Henri. Therefore a trap for Alphonse must be set. If he was found to be guilty, she must get rid of him.

She decided that Michel would need to be involved, so she arranged a meeting with him in the barn of the safe house.

'I want your help in setting a trap to prove conclusively that Alphonse is an informer.' Michel looked at Sandra a little incredulously as she spoke.

'Are you serious? I've known Alphonse for a long time. He can't be an informer. You've got it wrong. He's a good man.'

Sandra spoke firmly. 'Well, if what you say is true then my plan will confirm it, will it not?'

Michel looked resigned. He had indeed known Alphonse for a good time and had never doubted him. But he had to go along with Sandra. They had to find out if he was an informer.

'What is your plan?' asked Michel.

'We will have a meeting, just you, Alphonse and me. We will discuss a number of issues – future plans, what supplies we need from London and other things – and then I will outline where a new SOE agent is to be contacted in the village at Café Renoir, and at what time. I will say this agent is key to our future operations. Hopefully, Alphonse will swallow the bait and inform the Gestapo. We then have to arrange for a completely innocent person to be in Café Renoir, where they will be surprised and arrested by the Gestapo – and hopefully eventually released – thereby proving Alphonse is the informer.'

'Who will be this "completely innocent" person?' Michel asked.

'That's where you come in. I want you to let it be known to just one or two individuals that the café is having a wine-tasting hour – for free. That should bring some people along at the right time. Nothing else need be said. The only problem might be that too many people will turn up, making it all appear a bit silly, so make sure you don't let anyone know until just before the event. Are you all right with the plan?'

'Yes,' said Michel. 'It sounds good. And if I am confronted afterwards as to how I knew there was to be a wine-tasting hour, I will refer to some overheard conversation I must have misheard.'

'That sounds reasonable,' said Sandra. 'I think we have covered all eventualities. When shall we meet Alphonse?'

'How about this evening, in the barn?'

'Great, say at 6:30pm.'

Sandra and Michel were sat either side of a hay bale when Alphonse entered the barn. He was alone.

'*Bonsoir*,' said Alphonse as he sat down with them. 'What do you want to talk about?'

Sandra replied, '*Bonsoir* and thank you for coming, Alphonse. We wanted to let you know what is happening tomorrow night at Café Renoir, because we need you to be there to meet an SOE agent who will have just arrived from England. The meeting is scheduled for 7pm. The agent will identify himself using the password "De Gaulle" when proposing a toast. We need you then to identify yourself and lead him off to the church gates on the other side of the square from the café, where he will be collected. Is all that clear?'

'Yes. Perfectly clear. I will make sure I am there before 7pm.

Can you give me some idea of what the agent will look like?'

'I'm afraid not,' replied Sandra. 'We don't know any details like that.'

Alphonse thanked them both and got up to leave. Michel took him outside and bade him farewell.

Michel and Sandra continued talking after Alphonse had left and agreed they would hide themselves in the house opposite Café Renoir. If they saw any sign of the Gestapo, they would know Alphonse had indeed been a Nazi sympathiser or perhaps even a member of the traitorous Milice, an organisation of Frenchmen that were colluding with the Nazis.

Café Renoir was very quiet. It was about 6.45pm. The owner, Monsieur Henrique, was quietly reading a newspaper while he sat behind the bar waiting for customers to enter. There were only two customers in the café, both sat at tables. One was Alphonse, sitting in the corner where he had a view of the whole café.

Monsieur Henrique did not have long to wait for more customers. The door opened and in walked a tall man with a woman on his arm. He had never seen them before.

'Good evening,' he said. 'What can I get for you?'

'We have come for the wine-tasting. I trust you have some good local wines for us to try.'

Henrique was surprised. 'Wine-tasting? Who told you that? There is no wine-tasting planned for tonight. You must be mistaken.'

The tall man seemed a bit upset at the owner's response and retorted, 'Well, I hope not. We have cycled some three miles to be here. We were told that you would be opening a number of bottles for tasting. Surely we could try at least a few? We might even buy one.'

Henrique thought for a second and said, 'Very well. Just for you and your wife. Let me pour you both a drink.' He reached behind the bar and produced a bottle of red wine. Expertly removing the cork in seconds, he poured two glasses, each about a quarter full, and offered them to the couple, who took them eagerly and tasted the wine.

'That is excellent. What wine is it?' the woman asked as she savoured the sweet, dark liquid.

'It is Chateau De Papier' 37. One of my favourites,' responded Henrique.

The ensuing conversation between the owner and the new customers caused both Alphonse and the customer sitting near the door to join in and ask to sample the wine. After a few minutes of largesse from Henrique, all concerned seemed to be enjoying themselves very well.

Then the door opened and in walked two leather-clad Gestapo agents, one of whom shouted, 'Stay where you are! No one move!'

The other agent had produced his pistol and was pointing it at the group by the bar.

'Produce your identity papers at once. Hand them over for inspection. You first.' The Gestapo agent pointed at the tall man, who had replaced his wine glass on the bar.

'What is going on? Here are my papers.'

'And here are mine,' said his wife as they handed them over to the agent.

The Gestapo officer examined the identification documents and, apparently satisfied, handed them back.

'Why are you here?' he asked them.

'We have come for the free wine-tasting. We have done nothing wrong.'

'Free wine-tasting? You are not serious. You will be arrested and taken for further questioning. Raise your hands.'

They both did as they were told. The two Gestapo agents, both now with their pistols covering the man and his wife, marched them out into the street where they were put into a waiting car, which then drove off.

Opposite the café, Sandra and Michel saw everything that happened. It was all the proof required to prove that Alphonse was indeed a Nazi informer. How were they going to handle him? Sandra spoke first.

'We will have to dispose of him, Michel. He is a major threat to all our agents and the Maquis. He knows enough to hang the lot of us. Let's do it now.'

'Yes, but is there any way we can use him to our advantage? Could we give him false information to pass on to the Gestapo?'

'Sounds good, but for how long? They will soon discover the couple they have arrested are innocent. Then what? No, I think the sooner we get rid of Alphonse, the better. He must know the names of many other Maquis as well as ours, and he knows the location of some safe houses. We can't take the risk that he won't disclose this information to the Germans, if he hasn't already. We must get rid of him now!'

Michel thought for a few seconds and then nodded in agreement.

'How shall we do it?' he asked.

Sandra was not one to hang about.

'Leave it to me. Let's wait until he leaves the café, then follow him, and at a suitable point I will shoot him. The body must be disposed of – we can't take the risk of the Germans finding it and leaping to conclusions. We must bury him where he will not be found.'

'Come on then,' said Michel. He was looking out the window across the street to the café. Alphonse had just come out and was walking along the street away from their hiding place. They quickly gathered up the few things they had and followed him. After a few hundred yards, Alphonse turned right and walked down a narrow alleyway towards the outskirts of the village. He seemed very much at ease. He was thinking that the Gestapo must reward him for his information. It was not every day that two Resistance agents were captured by the Gestapo.

Michel and Sandra had separated. Michel followed Alphonse at a distance, while Sandra went on by a different route, hoping to get in front of Alphonse, stop him at the right time and do the necessary. Alphonse reached the end of the narrow alleyway, turned to the left and walked up a hill that would take him out of the village. He was heading back to his rooms that were some two miles away. He was in no hurry.

Sandra had managed to get ahead of Alphonse and was watching him climb the hill. She was near the top and had got out her pistol. There was no one else around that she could see.

As Alphonse drew level with her hiding place, she stepped out, pointing her pistol straight at him, and said, 'Stop. Don't move. I have something to say to you.'

He looked very surprised and asked, 'Sandra! *Mon amie.* Why are you holding that pistol? What is wrong?'

She met his gaze and replied, 'You know what is wrong. You have been betraying us and the Maquis. Just how many have you sent to their deaths? You are beneath contempt.'

'Sandra! You are wrong. I have betrayed no one. Where is your proof?'

'You were the only one who knew what was supposed to happen at the café tonight. We told no one else. And, sure enough, the Gestapo arrived and arrested two innocent people. We set this trap to catch you, and it worked.'

Alphonse's expression changed. He realised he had been duped and now exposed. How could he get out of this? This was just a woman standing in front of him. He would soon get her out of his way, he thought.

Sandra looked past Alphonse and down the hill. Michel had arrived on the scene and was walking up towards where they were standing. Sandra called to him and, with that momentary distraction, took her eyes off Alphonse. He moved like lightning, suddenly pulling his pistol out from under his jacket and raising it towards Sandra. She reacted immediately. Her mind was made up for her by his actions. She pulled the trigger of her pistol twice, hitting Alphonse in the chest and in the head. He spun on his feet and fell backwards in a heap.

Michel came running up the hill. Alphonse was dead.

'Well, he won't be grassing anyone up again,' Sandra commented as Michel arrived. 'Let's get rid of his body.'

Together they dragged his body away from the hill into a secluded spot next to a small cluster of trees. They had to dispose of him quickly to minimise any further action if the Gestapo found him.

'See if there is a spade anywhere,' said Sandra as she went through Alphonse's pockets, removing everything she could find. She placed it all in a small bag she had brought with her. She would examine all of Alphonse's bits and pieces in detail later, certain that they would contain something incriminating.

Michel had found a spade in a nearby garden and he began digging a hole next to one of the trees. Alphonse was soon buried under a foot of soil, which they stamped flat and covered with stones and bits of twigs. When they had completed their task, Michel and Sandra headed for their safe house at the farm.

The following day, Michel received information that the Gestapo had released the married couple arrested at the café. Of course they would now be looking for Alphonse to find out why he had given them false information. They would never find him. Sandra and Michel had resolved not to tell anyone, even Henri and Charles, what they had done. Any future questions regarding Alphonse's whereabouts would be met with a shrug of the shoulders and a 'Not seen him.'

Michel could only marvel to himself about Sandra. She had eliminated the traitor hiding in the midst of his sector of the Maquis. Many previously failed operations by the Maquis could now be explained. Alphonse had been a collaborator and sent many Maquis to their deaths. Sandra was very special indeed. He had never met anyone like her in his life. What a woman! he thought.

It was a few days after the elimination of Alphonse. Sandra was alone in the barn of the safe house. She had just finished her breakfast and was looking forward to Charles taking her out for dinner at a nearby restaurant that evening. Of course this was his recompense for having doubted Sandra's ability, leadership and determination, and for referring to her as 'only a woman'. Oh, she would make him pay for that remark! She was determined to drink as much expensive wine as possible during their meal.

The door at the rear of the barn opened and in came Michel. Sandra was expecting him. They had planned this meeting to discuss the possible consequences of the death of Alphonse, particularly from the Milice, and future actions by the Maquis.

'Sandra. Good to see you. Did you have a good night's sleep?'

'I did, thank you. It is so peaceful here. All I hear is the lovely sound of the birds calling that wakes me up in the morning. And then I am treated to a lovely breakfast by Claudette. Do you know, sometimes I feel as if I'm almost on holiday? Sometimes.'

'Glad to hear it. The French countryside is delightful, as you have discovered. Now, shall we get down to business?'

'Good idea. Before we discuss plans, weren't you going to tell me a little more about the Milice?'

'Yes, of course. Well, the Milice are a paramilitary force created early last year by the Vichy regime to help the Germans fight the French Resistance. They have authorised executions and assassinations of Maquis, and they helped the Nazis round up Jews and others throughout France for deportation to Germany. And, as you know from the trap set for Alphonse, they work hand in glove with the Gestapo. They are despised as traitors by all true Frenchmen. They are not as easy to avoid as the Germans because they are French and have lived in the area in which they operate for most of their lives. Therefore, they are better at spotting newcomers and detecting agents speaking French with an unusual accent. And, believe it or not, they are paid by the Germans.'

'Paid! By the Nazis?' Sandra was incredulous.

'Yes. Paid, in Francs.'

Sandra was quite shocked by this. She knew something of the Milice from her training with the SOE in England. But she had no idea of the extent of their activity and how treacherous they were to their homeland. Michel's short summary of their activities showed them to be deplorable.

'What can we expect them to do once they are aware that Alphonse is no longer to be found? Will they try to replace him with someone else?'

'Most certainly,' said Michel. 'We must be very aware of anyone who tries to get involved in our activities. Trust no one.'

'Too true,' agreed Sandra. 'Now, let's get on to our next operation. London wants us to destroy some of the railway links between Rouen and Paris as soon as possible. I have no doubt our actions here will help shorten the war. Is there somewhere we could meet the local Maquis in that area and get them to help carry out the plan?'

'Yes,' replied Michel. 'The best place would be at the church in the village of Mèche St Laurent. It's about twenty miles from here. We could cycle there in about three hours, mostly through the woods, to avoid detection. I can arrange a meeting there for tomorrow night. Is that OK with you?'

'Certainly. Tomorrow night would be fine. How many Maquis would you expect to turn up?'

'About a dozen. We should not have a very long meeting with them. If you prepare the plan of action and assure them of receiving plenty of supplies from London to carry out their attacks, they will be satisfied. I have dealt with some of them before. I think they can be trusted.'

'Well, that sounds reasonable, Michel. What time do you think we should leave here tomorrow to reach Mèche St Laurent?'

'Around 6pm. I will arrange the meeting for midnight, so we will get there in plenty of time. We will have to travel back here immediately after the meeting, so we won't get much sleep tomorrow night. Are you OK with that?'

'Yes. Of course. Sounds a good plan to me. I'll just get on and draw some plans for them to look at tomorrow night.'

'And I will leave now and contact them to arrange our meeting. Have you anything else planned for today?'

'Not today. No. I do have a busy evening ahead of me, however. Claudette is lending me one of her very best dresses so that I look nice, and she has even managed to find some make-up for me to put on and improve my looks, including – can you believe? – lipstick, real lipstick! I can't wait to put it on. It will be such a change from using beetroot to brighten up one's lips!'

'My! Who's the lucky person going out with you tonight?'

'Charles. It's to make up for the comment he made about me being "only a woman". You remember, surely.'

'Of course. I hope you have a very enjoyable evening. Send Charles my best. And don't drink too much. We have a busy day tomorrow.'

'Don't worry about my drinking, but I will drink him under the table. And we will be drinking the more expensive vintages. He will pay heavily for his remarks!'

'Certainly sounds like it. See you tomorrow.'

Michel left by the rear door of the barn, leaving Sandra to

prepare for the meeting the next day. He almost felt sorry for Charles. It was going to be, he thought, a very expensive evening for him. He felt sure it would be worth it, however, having the lovely Sandra for company.

Sandra finished preparing the plans for her meeting with the Maquis. She was meeting Charles at the restaurant at 6pm and wanted to be ready in good time. Later, she put on the loveliest blue and white dress, and Claudette helped her with her hair. Finally, Sandra applied the real lipstick.

She was ready for action!

Chapter 7

'Can I get you something to drink?'

The waitress looked at Charles as she spoke, but the reply came from Sandra.

'Thank you. We will have a bottle of Châteauneuf-du-Pape '38 to begin with.'

Charles tried to look pleased, but his thoughts were now mainly about how much this meal with Sandra would cost him. How he wished he had not made those senseless, thoughtless comments, especially since she had proved beyond doubt with her subsequent actions – particularly the rescue of Coles from Rouen Tower – just what a brave, resourceful leader she was.

The waitress brought the wine and poured a little into the glass on Charles' right. He tasted it and nodded to the waitress, who then poured them a full glass each.

'This is a very nice wine. Thank you for the meal. It is so nice of you to take me to Duets – I've never been here before.'

'My pleasure. It's the least I could do after making those stupid remarks to you. Let's just enjoy ourselves!'

Sandra and Charles did their very best to relax and enjoy the evening together. Unusually, there was no one in uniform in the restaurant. This made things much easier from a conversational point of view. They had also requested a secluded corner so that it would be difficult for them to be overheard by anyone. Charles knew the owner very well. He was a man they could trust and he had helped them many times recently. Eventually, their conversation turned towards what further plans were to be carried out to disrupt the occupying forces, but Sandra quickly brought this to an end. It was not the time or place to discuss tactics.

She concluded by whispering to Charles, 'We will have a meeting tomorrow night at the church in the village of Mèche St Laurent. We have arranged to meet some members of the local Maquis there. Michel will be attending and I would like you to be there. That's enough. Oh, and have you noticed that our bottle of Châteauneuf-du-Pape is empty? Please could we have another one?'

Sandra's eyes were twinkling and Charles, naturally, ordered another bottle. The conversation became more light-hearted as the evening wore on. They enjoyed each other's company. It was a welcome relief from their day-to-day activities in the Resistance. Sandra was sorry when the evening came to an end as the waiter began clearing the empty tables and preparing them for the following day.

Sandra had to be honest, though, that she felt no sexual

attraction to Charles. She would not be continuing their get-together after leaving the restaurant. No, she would be heading straight to the safe house for a good night's sleep in preparation for the following day's work. She did notice, however, the slight disappointment on Charles' face when she declared she would be heading straight from Duets to the safe house. Well, at least he is disappointed, she thought with a sense of elation. After parting with Charles, having thanked him for the lovely meal and wished him Godspeed, Sandra headed towards Claudette's place, walking quickly. She would be sleeping in her usual abode in the small hut at the back of the main house. She felt safe there.

The church at the village of Mèche St Laurent was very old. It had served the local community for almost 800 years and was very dear to the villagers, who used it often as a meeting place, as well as a place of worship. Sandra's plan was to meet the Maquis in the church and decide the best course of action for dealing with the rail links that were nearby.

Michel had accompanied her to the church. They had travelled by bike the twenty or more miles from the safe house during the day and were both glad to stop and have a rest in the church pews. Sandra marvelled at the interior. The stained-glass windows, the wonderfully carved pew ends, the ornate stone pulpit and the carved wooden rood screen – all contributing to a serene interior that gave her the feeling of being in a very safe as well as holy place.

Michel turned towards Sandra as they sat together in the pew and said, 'When the Maquis arrive, I expect around a dozen to turn up. I will open the meeting and introduce you to them.

Some of them may find it difficult to deal with you because you are female. They are just not used to it! So please be patient with them.'

'Don't worry. I will be patient. I am getting used to some of the more, shall I say, anti-women comments from some of your colleagues. Once we have got over the initial hurdles, I will outline which parts of the rail network we want sabotaged and when. And I will be able to tell them what supplies we can arrange to be dropped from London for them to collect and use. I hope they will be pleased!'

'I hope so, too,' agreed Michel.

Their conversation was interrupted by the sound of the main church door opening, followed by murmurings of conversation as the members of the Maquis entered the church and sat down in the pews. They left one man to guard the door.

Sandra and Michel stood up, and Michel welcomed them and introduced Sandra. The Maquis, who numbered ten and were all male, listened closely. When Michel finished speaking, the man sitting nearest to him spoke. He introduced himself as Nathan and was obviously the leader of this Maquis team. All the other members seemed quite happy to let him do all the talking.

'Thank you for this meeting, Michel,' he said, 'and welcome to you, Sandra. We have much to ask you. But please tell us why you need us, and what plans have you got in store?'

Nathan was a short man, dressed in a long overcoat, which no doubt concealed his pistol.

Sandra replied, 'Thank you very much, Nathan. It is an honour to be here with you. I have to tell you all that I know, which is that, following the invasion of France by the Allied forces, we can expect them to be very soon fighting their way towards where we are sat here. I do not know any dates for this, but I believe they will not be long in coming. Because of this, it is supremely important that people like you, the Maquis, are ready to carry out as much sabotage and create as much disruption to the occupying forces as possible. That is why I am here. I can ensure that you get plenty of the necessary supplies and equipment from London that you will need to disrupt the rail links all around this area, and help prevent reinforcements being brought up by the Germans that might limit the movement and advance of our Allied troops.'

'Tell us what you want us to do,' Nathan exhorted her. Several of the other Maquis had also been making noises of encouragement in response to Sandra's opening remarks. There was no doubt in Michel's mind that what Sandra had said and the way she had said it had captured the fighting spirit of the Maquis. What a woman!

The meeting continued with Sandra and Michel producing a map of the area showing the train routes and highlighting the places where they wanted the most commotion to be caused. Questions came thick and fast, particularly from Nathan, concerning locations and times of attack. All of these Sandra could answer very well. A list of the supplies they required was produced. Sandra was able to assure them that their requirements would be dropped the following night by the RAF at a location she and Michel had already agreed would be best. The Maquis supported all they said. It had been a very successful meeting. The sabotage of the railway tracks would take place the night following the drop. Sandra told Nathan where they would meet and that she would be on her own leading the attack. Michel was going to remain in the safe house and await Sandra's return after the tracks had been destroyed.

After about two hours, when just about all the necessary

business had been completed, Nathan stood up and thanked Sandra and Michel on behalf of them all, promising they would do all within their power to achieve the successful outcome of Sandra's plan. There was almost a sense of euphoria in the church, which could be felt by them all. The Maquis had spent the last four years since the German invasion trying to come to terms with the lack of progress in removing the hostile force from their land. Now there was something tangible happening: an agent from England in front of them talking and leading, the expected drop of ammunition and equipment from London, and the planned attack to help them defeat the enemy. The hope of a coming victory following the Allied invasion of Normandy had made them feel elated. It had felt such a long time coming.

Nathan asked everyone present to bow their heads for a short prayer. He then said, 'Dear Lord. Thank you for bringing us safely here. We ask for your help now in defeating our enemy. Give us guidance over the next few days and keep us safe in your hands. In Jesus' name we pray. Amen.'

Everyone responded with 'Amen'. The Maquis then left the church quietly. Sandra and Michel waited for a few minutes before they locked the church door and got on their bikes for the journey back to the safe house.

The next morning brought rain to the countryside around the safe house. Sandra and Michel had agreed to meet after breakfast and cycle to the small village some miles away where Nathan lived. It was from here that they were going to take Nathan and a few others to the zone where London had agreed to drop the promised supplies: explosives, ammunition and guns for the Maquis to use in their forthcoming sabotage action. They reached the village at about midday and were soon talking with Nathan.

'How far is the drop zone from here?' Nathan asked Sandra.

'Not far. We could be there in half an hour. The plan is to drop the supplies around midnight. We must not get there too early. Of course we'll need some of your men to help collect the supplies as they are dropped. We will also need them to light flares to guide the plane in.'

'That's no problem. I will arrange all that, but please avoid showing yourself around the village. It's best if you stay here and don't go out.'

'Yes, of course, but why? There are no German troops in the area. Surely we wouldn't be in trouble if we went to the local café for a meal?'

'Our problem is with the Milice. We know there are members of the Milice in this area, and they would easily spot anything or anyone unusual and tell their German friends about it. We know this to be the case. We have to be very careful. There were a few Jewish families living in the village until last year. The Milice informed on them and helped the Nazi troops round them up. As far as we know, all the families were sent to Germany and since then no one has heard anything. We fear the worst for them. Many were just children.'

Michel looked at Nathan and Sandra and said, 'Of course we will stay here until dark, then we can all leave and reach the drop zone in plenty of time. But do you know who the Milice are? Where they live or anything about them?'

Nathan hesitated, then replied, 'We know who some of them are, yes. We have not, so far, taken it upon ourselves to begin a fight with them, mainly because we do not know what the consequences might be. We try hard not to let them know anything about us. If they did find out about our activities, the Nazis would take over and wipe us out – with the help of the Milice, no doubt. They are all French and, as far as we are concerned, all traitors. They have been brainwashed into believing that Nazism is a good thing for our country. They will pay the price of their treachery one day when we are free.'

Michel was well aware of the Milice in his own area of operation. They could never be trusted. He said, 'We will have our revenge on them soon.'

Sandra now understood more about the Milice and their treachery, and now she was getting closer to them she could feel the Maquis' hatred for them. She tried to imagine a similar situation happening in England, if the planned Nazi invasion had been carried out after Dunkirk, but she could not.

The following evening it was very dark. There was no moon that night and the grass they were lying on was a little wet from the day's rain.

Sandra whispered, 'It looks all clear. I think we can plant our charges now. Spread them as far as possible along the railway, keeping the next person in view, and when we are all done I shall signal to set the detonators for five minutes. We must then make our way as far as possible from the railway. There is no need to meet up. Just get back to your safe places as fast as you can. Are we all clear on what needs to be done?'

There was a general mumble of assent. Sandra was surrounded by about ten Maquis, most of whom had attended the meeting in the church at the village of Mèche St Laurent. They were ready. The plan was to destroy at least a quarter of a mile of track, which should cause enough disruption to the network to distract the Germans. It would take them a long time to re-lay the tracks.

'Let's go! Good luck, everyone,' said Sandra.

Everyone moved forward quickly with their explosives in hand. They spread out along the straight section of track, where each one could see the adjacent Maquis. They quickly planted the explosives and fixed the detonators. Sandra waited until they had all signalled by indicating to the next in line down the track until the closest to her waved to say all the detonators were in place. She then gave a long, shrill whistle, indicating that the detonators be activated. Once all was completed, the Maquis quickly ran away from the tracks towards their safe places.

Sandra then dashed to where she had hidden her bike, behind a hedge a little way down the road that ran parallel with the railway. She was on her own and was determined to get back to safety as soon as possible. This was the first time since she had been in France that she had completed an operation without the assistance of Michel. He was staying in the safe house, awaiting her return.

As Sandra reached where she had hidden her bike the sound of the charges exploding shattered the comparative silence. The noise continued for at least ten seconds as the different detonators triggered the explosions until all the charges had performed their job and, all being well, destroyed the tracks. Another successful operation, hoped Sandra. She knew the degree of success would be confirmed the following day when a Maquis would check and report on the amount of damage. She felt jubilant.

Sandra quickly pulled her bike from the clump of bushes and

began to cycle the six miles back to Claudette's place. She would try to avoid the roads and keep in the nearby woods where possible. She was certain that the area would soon be crawling with German troops arriving to investigate the damage and she did not want them to see her. Cycling through woods was not easy. So many trees, bushes and stones, and a lack of any defined track made for a difficult journey. It was going to take at least three or four hours for Sandra to get to safety. It would be daylight by the time she reached home.

'Keep going, keep going, pedal, pedal, and come on!' Sandra repeated to herself as she got closer to safety. It was now almost dawn and she had managed to make almost the whole journey without using the roads at all. There was only about another half a mile to go. 'Keep going, keep going, just a bit more effort! Nearly there now!' She was concentrating so much on the effort needed that she failed to spot the two German soldiers stopped just by the roadside, near to where she was cycling. They had set up a road barrier to check any traffic that might be implicated in the destruction of the railway tracks. Unfortunately, her bike hit a stone and as it jumped into the air, Sandra fell on to the ground with a yell. She lay there with the bike on top of her and her legs wrapped around the frame. The noise she made attracted the two German soldiers, one of whom came over to where she lay and pointed his rifle at her, demanding that she stand up.

Bugger it, thought Sandra. All this way and then this happens! She would have to play the part of a demure Frenchwoman to get out of this. The German soldier waved his gun at her and then pointed it in the direction of his colleague. She would have to comply.

'*Schnell, schnell!*' he said loudly as she tried to push her bike towards the road where the other German soldier was waiting. Eventually, she reached him and saw that he too had his rifle pointing at her. This was not looking good, she thought.

'*Vos papiers?*'

The second German knew some French at least. Sandra reached inside her jacket and produced her identity papers, which were read and handed back to her without comment. She put them back in her jacket and motioned to get back on her bike and ride off, but the soldier's rifle shoved in her side stopped her immediately.

'*Levez vos mains.*' ('Raise your hands.')

Sandra had no alternative but to do as she was told. They would now find her gun and that would be it. Handcuffed and off for interrogation by the Gestapo, no doubt. She had to do something pretty quickly.

As the soldier reached inside her jacket and began searching, Sandra stepped back slightly and positioned herself so she could bring her right hand down from its elevated position and chop the soldier across his neck just below his ear. He fell to the ground and stayed there. His colleague began to raise his rifle to aim at Sandra, who, reaching inside her jacket, whipped out her pistol and pointed it at the German soldier at the same time. She pulled the trigger and dropped sideways, pulling the trigger again. The soldier's rifle went off, and Sandra felt the bullet graze her arm as she fell. The soldier collapsed to the ground with two bullets in his chest.

Sandra got up and checked the soldier she had chopped across the neck. He was dead. Her training had worked. She had killed a Nazi with her bare hands! Leaving the two dead soldiers where they lay, she quickly got on her bike and pedalled furiously back into the woods for the last few hundred yards towards the safe house. It would not be long before the bodies would be discovered and there would be a search of the whole area by the Germans. She must warn everyone. It had been a narrow escape.

Chapter 8

Sandra and Michel shared the last drop of Calvados. It was now 7pm and Sandra had spent the time since reaching safety trying to relax a little. The bottle was the only one left from the small stock kept hidden in the safe house. At least that was what Claudette said. The last bottle. Funny how almost magically these bottles seemed to appear! Sandra told Michel what had happened half a mile away to the two soldiers, and they agreed that this would probably mean just about every house in the district being searched by the Nazis.

With the last drop they toasted 'absent friends', of whom there were many. The last few weeks had been very dangerous, busy and full of experiences that would stay with both of them for the rest of their lives. They drained their glasses with a sigh.

'What next?' Michel asked.

Sandra replied immediately. 'We have received a message from London. Bobby Coles is to be sent back to England, along with two RAF pilots who escaped from their POW camp. They are at a safe house near Montigny, awaiting our signal to join us here so we can take them to the pick-up point. At the same time, London is sending over three agents, one of whom is an explosive expert, to help us accelerate our sabotage of German communications. The Lysander with the agents on board will be landing tomorrow night. We must get everything ready for the changeover.'

'Right,' said Michel. 'I will get Bobby to the landing field if you will send the signal to the safe house. It shouldn't take the two RAF chaps long to get here, probably around two hours. We can then all go to the landing field and prepare.'

They said goodbye to each other and went about the business of ensuring another successful changeover, and the safe return of Bobby and the RAF pilots.

The next day, Michel and Sandra met in the late afternoon near the landing field. They had got Bobby and the RAF pilots together the previous evening and ensured they had the necessary food and clothes to help them get home. The weather was not good. It had been raining almost continuously for the previous few hours. Though that had stopped now, it was still very muddy in the fields around the landing area. The five of them sheltered under some trees while they waited for the drone of the Lysander's Mercury engine, which they knew would come shortly after the moon reached a reasonable level of brightness as the night progressed. Conversation while they waited was full of their shared adventures. Sandra spent much of the time listening to the two RAF pilots, who couldn't wait to be off back home. They had some interesting stories to tell regarding their incarceration and both Bobby and Michel had also been listening with interest. Sandra kept looking up to the sky. She was the first to hear it, the unmistakable noise of the Mercury engine.

'Quick! Light the flares,' she called to the others, who went and did what they had planned earlier in the day. The Lysander did a circuit around the landing area to make certain it was the correct place, and then slowly and deliberately came down towards where the five of them were waiting.

'Steady, my boy!' murmured one of the pilots, looking upwards. 'Steady!'

He needn't have worried. The Lysander pilot knew exactly what he was doing as he brought the plane down into the flare-marked field and landed easily. He eased the plane to a stop at the same time as turning it through a semi-circle so as to be facing the right way for a speedy take-off and departure back to Blighty. They all rushed towards the plane. They could see the rear canopy being thrown back and three figures climbing out of the plane, making their way over the edge and down the ladder fixed to the Lysander. By the time they reached the plane, the three agents were on the ground.

One agent turned towards Sandra and said, '*L'usine a tarte est-elle proche d'ici ?*' ('Is the pie factory near here?')

She responded with the appropriate password code.

'*Non. C'est sur la colline.*' ('No. It is over the hill.')

The three evacuees clambered up the ladder into the Lysander's cramped cockpit. They were soon aboard. Sandra and Michel waved them off and turned back into the cover of the nearby woods as the Lysander's engine began increasing its revs for take-off. Sandra, Michel and the three new agents reached the comparative safety of the woods and turned to see the Lysander as it took off. To their surprise and concern, it had not moved. Its engine was racing, but it had not moved.

'Oh no! Something's gone wrong. I'll go back and find out what it is. You stay here.' With that, Michel sprinted across the wet field towards the plane, where he was met by the voice of the pilot shouting down from his cockpit, 'It's stuck in the mud! We will need help to push us out.'

Michel could see the problem. The Lysander's front wheels had sunk into the soft mud where it had come to a stop. The heavy rain of recent days had caused this particular part of the landing field to become especially boggy. The Lysander was not going to get out of the mire without some help to push the plane forward. Emergency action was called for.

Michel beckoned to Sandra and the other agents to come and help, which they did, running across the field. They all got behind the wheel struts and tried to push the plane out of the mud, but to no avail. What were they going to do?

Sandra said to the agents around her, 'We will need more people to help. It's risky. However, there's nothing for it but to enlist the help of some of the villagers or the plane will never take off. Tie some ropes around the undercarriage.' She sent Michel off to the village to try to get some help. In the meantime, all they could do was wait and hope. The pilot of the Lysander got out of his cockpit and stood by a wing. It was at this point that Sandra noticed the pilot was James Silverstone.

'Well, we meet again.'

James looked up and a smile of recognition lit up his face. 'It's not? Yes, it is! So good to see you, and after all you went through. It's just wonderful that you're alive!'

James walked over and embraced Sandra. She enjoyed the feeling of his strong arms about her.

'How on earth did you survive? Please tell me.'

'I was very, very lucky,' she said. 'Although my parachute didn't open, I hit some trees on the way down. The branches were not very thick, so they just broke away as I passed down through them, and they slowed me up sufficiently that when I hit the ground I wasn't killed, just winded. The good Lord was watching over me. There can be no other explanation.'

'But didn't the branches cause you some injury? Or did they all just bend out of the way?'

'Well, not quite,' replied Sandra. 'You see, the trees that saved me were a group of Blue Atlas Cedar trees that I was lucky enough to land on. Their branches are small at the top and become stronger as you go down. They cushioned my fall progressively as I fell earthwards. I did sustain a number of bruises that took some time to heal, but I'm OK now. I really believe it was a miracle.'

'Well, you may be right there! You are extremely lucky to have survived. Anyway, it's good to hear.'

Sandra smiled at James and said, 'But there is one thing that fall has made me realise about staying alive.'

'Oh yes, and what is that?'

'I will never, ever jump from a plane with a parachute on again! Never!'

The force with which Sandra said this left James and the others in no doubt that she meant it.

Their conversation was interrupted by the sound of voices coming from the corner of the field. They looked towards the source and could just make out Michel leading what looked like a sizeable group of people hurrying towards them.

'He's persuaded some villagers to come! Well done,' said James. 'I'll get back on board.'

James clambered up into his cockpit as Michel and the villagers lined themselves along each of the two ropes attached to the Lysander's undercarriage. Sandra waited until both ropes were taut and then shouted the order: 'Pull!'

Slowly, but surely, the plane began to move. There must have been at least thirty people on the ropes and another six or seven pushing the tailplane. It was a mighty effort. The engine was fired up as the plane moved forward until it was clear of the muddy section of the field. Sandra gave the order to stop pulling and the ropes were removed from the undercarriage. Everybody stood back and Sandra gave James the signal that he could now take off. The Lysander picked up speed and was soon bouncing along the field, then shortly lifted up into the sky, to the accompaniment of a loud cheer from the assembled crowd.

'Thank you all. *Merci, merci, merci,*' Sandra called out to all around as the noise from the Lysander drummed in the distance. Michel echoed her thanks to all who had helped, then implored them all to return home as soon as possible.

It had been a very eventful night. Sandra, Michel and the three new agents made their way from the field towards the safe house, which they reached after a couple of hours walking through the woods. On the way there, the new agents revealed that they were from three different groups. One was an SOE agent named

Matthew Poulston and he was in command. The second was an American who gave his name as Bill Lunden and was a member of the American Office of Strategic Services (OSS), while the third was a Frenchman, Adam Bisset, who belonged to the Free French Bureau Central de Renseignements et d'Action (Central Bureau of Intelligence and Action). They had much to tell Sandra and Michel, including information concerning which targets had to be attacked and how soon. There would be a long conversation once they had achieved the safety of the farmhouse.

Once they reached the farmhouse barn, both Sandra and Michel were surprised to find that, under their overcoats, all three newcomers were in uniform. Michel commented that this was very unusual. He had never known it before during all his time in the Resistance.

'Why are you all in uniform? Surely this is not good if you are going to try to remain under cover?' asked Michel.

'Good point,' said Poulston. 'Allow me to explain.'

Sandra and Michel listened attentively.

'Since the invasion, it has been decided by the powers that be that the British, the Americans and the French should work together when carrying out undercover operations in France. That is why the three of us are here together. We are one of the first teams to be airlifted in under the code name for this initiative. We are what is known as a "Jedburgh" team. Please don't ask me why they have given us that name. I don't know, though I would hope there is a logical reason for it. Each team will have a leader and a communications expert, as well as other skills, of course, including expertise in the use of explosives. Our remit is to co-ordinate activity with existing SOE agents and the Maquis to cause further disruption to the German lines of communication.'

'Wonderful!' exclaimed Sandra. 'But why are you in uniform?'

'Oh, yes. Well, it was decided that all Jedburgh teams dropped into France would be in uniform so that, if captured by the Germans, they would be treated as prisoners of war and not tortured and shot as spies.'

This last comment was received by Michel and Sandra with slight looks of scepticism. Doubtfully, Sandra said, 'Sounds reasonable, I suppose, though I admire your belief that the Germans will play by the rules of the game. That is not our experience at all.'

Michel was quick to add his own comment. 'I can give you a recent example of the most appalling murders of innocent men by the Germans as retribution for the escape of one of our agents. This took place in a village near here. I'm afraid you might find it rather unbelievable.'

'Not at all. Please tell us what happened.' This request came from the Frenchman, Adam Bisset, who went on to explain that he knew this area very well as he had lived here with his parents for many years.

Michel said, 'Then I am afraid you may find this very upsetting. Do you know the village of Bourg-Achard?'

'Why, yes. My parents had a house just a few miles from there. I had a few friends who lived there, and they probably still do.'

Michel told the story of the escape of Bobby Coles and the subsequent revenge taken by the Nazis upon the men of Bourg-Achard. The increasingly incredulous looks on the faces of the three members of the Jedburgh team told its own story.

Poulston was the first to speak when Michel finished. 'Is

this really true? I've never heard anything like it. Surely there must be some kind of mistake? Shooting innocent civilians in cold blood?'

Sandra was not a little dismayed at the naivety of Poulston's comments. During her SOE training, she had been told to expect many things. Surely Poulston's training would have been similar, she thought. Sandra had to admit, though, that retribution on the scale they'd witnessed – mass murder of innocent civilians by the Nazis – had not been mentioned. She knew that her experiences since arriving in occupied France had given her a much clearer understanding of the enemy.

Adam Bisset was next to speak. 'This is terrible. I knew the Germans were capable of many awful things, but this is beyond anything I'd imagined. Please can you take us to the village now? I must see what has happened. How far is it from here?'

'It's about six miles,' Michel replied. 'We could walk it in a couple of hours through the woods. That would be the safest way. We would have to be extra careful because of your uniforms. Let's have a bite to eat and then head off. It would be good to leave soon because we would be under cover of darkness the whole time. I suggest just you and Matthew do this with me. Sandra and Bill should stay here and wait for our return.'

Michel's suggestions were met with agreement by everyone. After the meal, Sandra said farewell as Michel, Adam and Matthew left to go to the stricken village. It was already fast approaching midnight and she did not expect them to return until late the next morning. After she had secured the door, she showed Bill where in the barn he could sleep for the night. Sandra then wished him goodnight and went out through the secret exit at the back of the barn to her little room in the outhouse. She was concerned about how Adam would react when he reached the village he had known before the war.

It was mid-morning the next day before Michel returned with Adam and Matthew, who both looked severely shaken by what they had seen and heard in the village. They explained to Bill the truth of the situation as they had seen it for themselves. They agreed that they should report it back to England. Adam said he would do that as soon as possible.

Matthew was the first among them to change the subject. 'There is to be a drop of supplies tonight. It will be a lot of ammunition, guns and other items. Can you arrange for some Maquis to help us collect it all? Of course we will also need their help to use it when we carry out our plans to disrupt the troop movements.'

'Certainly,' said Sandra. 'What is your plan after the drop?'

'We have been told in London that you, Sandra and Michel, have been more than competent in co-ordinating the Maquis, carrying out a number of raids that have disrupted much of the enemy's activity. The destruction of factories, train links and the Gestapo headquarters have all been vital to distract the enemy and contribute to the Allies' success in driving them back, thus assisting our advance. We thank you both for all that. There is, however, one other target that London wants destroyed as soon as is possible.'

'What is it?' interrupted Michel.

'It is the railway bridge at Barentin Viaduct that crosses the Austreberthe River on the Paris–Le Havre line near the town of Barentin in Normandy. It's about twelve miles from *Rouen*.'

'Couldn't the RAF bomb it?' asked Sandra.

'They have tried and failed in the past, but London thinks we could mount a more precise attack that would also reduce the number of civilian casualties in the area.'

'Sounds reasonable enough, but we will need masses of explosives to bring down that viaduct. It's huge!' Michel knew the viaduct well and could imagine how difficult it would be to destroy it.

'That is why we need your help this evening in collecting all the supplies that are going to be dropped from London. We are expecting approximately 1,500 pounds of explosives to be dropped. All of them must be collected and then transported to the viaduct in time to blow it up the day after tomorrow. We have been tasked to do this as quickly as possible.'

Sandra felt it was time to speak.

'OK. This is going to take some organising. We will need at least twenty Maquis to transport the explosives, unless we can get a van of some description to transport it all together. That may be possible. We know of a transport business in the village and it might be possible to use one of their trucks to move it. The viaduct is about thirty miles from here, so if you want it destroyed in two days we will have to move very quickly.'

'That's true,' agreed Michel. 'And we will need an expert to tell us where to plant the explosives so that they do the maximum damage and bring the viaduct down.'

'That's no problem. I am the trained explosives expert in our team. I will be there to direct where to plant the charges.' It was Bill Lunden, the American, who reassured everyone with this remark.

Michel said, 'I'll be responsible for getting the Maquis together. If we've finished here, I'll go and do that now.'

Later that evening, they all made their way to the drop zone where they met with the other Maquis, who had been told of the rendezvous and what was needed. There must have been at least two dozen agents scattered around the field where the explosives were due to land. They did not have long to wait. The drone of the Mercury engine powering the Lysander echoed through the night as it headed towards the flares lit by the Maquis to mark the drop zone.

'There are two of them! Look.' The shout from one of the Maquis was heard by Sandra and Michel, who strained their eyes to see in the dark sky. Sure enough, two Lysanders could be seen in the distance. Soon after, they caught sight of parachutes as they descended with their cargo into the drop zone. The planes immediately turned and had gone in minutes. The Maquis and the Jedburgh team quickly collected all the supplies and put them into the borrowed truck that had been procured to take everything to the viaduct. The Jedburgh team had decided to go with the explosives and supplies in the truck, while Sandra, Michel and the other Maquis preferred to cycle the thirty miles to their meeting place. They intended to do this the next day. Cycling at night was not the best way to avoid attention from the Nazis.

Michel and Sandra started their journey to Barentin Viaduct early the next morning. They planned to get there by late afternoon and meet up with the Jedburgh team to finalise the plan for how the destruction would be carried out the following day. The journey was uneventful and they reached Barentin just before 4pm.

After settling in, Michel sent a message to London giving them information about the progress of events. From all the different messages and information both Michel and Sandra were receiving from various sources, it was evident that the Allies were making good progress from Normandy. They hoped it would not be long before they were shaking hands with Allied troops.

They met with the Jedburgh team that evening and, with some of the local Maquis, formulated a plan of deployment and decided where to position the explosives. Bill Lunden went to great lengths to explain in which viaduct supports the charges were to be placed and how they were to be fixed to the structures to cause the maximum damage. Everyone knew exactly what was required of them for the following evening. The meeting broke up and they all returned to their resting places in anticipation.

'Are we ready?' Matthew Poulston's quiet request was met with agreement by everyone around. They were all at the base of one of the viaduct supports, but now the group split in two and half the team moved away to the adjacent support. Their plan was to destroy both supports at the same time. This would almost certainly cause the entire length of the viaduct to collapse. Sandra helped plant some explosives around the support and, when everything was finished, Matthew signalled to the other group that they were ready. He received a confirmation signal from the other group and they both set detonators for one hour's time, then made a hasty exit away from the towering viaduct.

Michel and Sandra reached their safe house about fifty minutes later. It was three miles from the viaduct, but they could still just about hear the muffled noise of the explosions when they came. They soon discovered, through reports from local Maquis, that the operation had been a success. The viaduct was destroyed. No German troops would be using that rail link to travel anywhere soon.

Sandra and Michel travelled back to Claudette's the next morning. From there, Sandra was to leave by train the next day to meet another SOE agent at a village station not far from Rouen, and plan further operations. She tried to get a good night's sleep before boarding the train, but her mind would not stop thinking. In the end, she got up at 5am and sat reading a French-language copy of *Les Misérables* until it was time for breakfast and to leave for the train, which fortunately was on a direct line that had not been sabotaged by the Resistance.

Michel accompanied Sandra to the village, where he took her bike and wished her Godspeed. She was going to walk the last few hundred yards to the station carrying her suitcase. As she left, she turned to look at Michel and said, '*Au revoir, mon ami.*'

Chapter 9

Sandra knew that this was the end. The Luger pistol pointing at her head was more than enough to make her stand still and await orders. The two Gestapo agents who had stopped her at the railway station knew exactly what they were doing. They quickly checked her identity papers and then tied her hands behind her back. The station was busy, but no one was going to interfere or come to Sandra's aid. No one intervened when Gestapo agents were arresting somebody. The general population had seen similar arrests before and would just want to keep out of trouble. The two agents pushed Sandra along the platform towards their car, which was parked outside the station.

The giveaway had been so simple it annoyed her. As she attempted to board the train, one of the Gestapo agents, who was stood behind her, had shouted in English with a definite Home Counties accent, 'Excuse me, but you've just dropped your purse!'

And, like a fool, Sandra had stopped, turned around and looked down at the platform for her purse.

The agent then said, 'Ah, so we can speak English! Put your hands up!' He produced his Luger pistol and pointed it at her head. The other agent came running down the platform and together they arrested Sandra.

Damn, damn, damn, she thought. What a fool to make such a stupid mistake! The two agents pushed her into the back of the car. While one sat alongside her, the other drove off, no doubt towards some Gestapo interrogation building. The journey was over in ten minutes and, once there, Sandra was first blindfolded and then bundled from the car into the headquarters and into a bare, cold room with no windows, in the middle of which was a chair to which she was tied, hands and feet.

This is it, she thought. This. Is. It.

Sandra was left alone in the room for what she imagined was a few hours. The agents had removed her blindfold, but she had no idea of the time. There was nothing around to give any indication. The only light came from a bulb hanging in the middle of the ceiling and it was very dim. How long will this last? she thought.

There was the sound of scuffling feet outside the door and the noise of keys being used. The door opened and in came two uniformed Gestapo men. They shut the door and the first German said in a thick accent, 'What is your real name?'

Sandra was at least prepared for this and replied, 'Joan Colline.

It's on my identity papers. You must have seen them. Why have you arrested me?'

'We ask the questions. You can speak English and are an agent for the English. So, why not admit it now and save yourself a lot of hardship?'

'No, I am not. You are wrong. Yes, I lived in England many years ago, but now I live in France and I work for Monsieur Le Castile at his café in Rue Madre. You can check it out if you don't believe me.'

'No, we don't believe you. The sooner you admit you are a British agent the better.'

At this point, the second German raised his arm and threw his hand across Sandra's face. She cried out in pain. The assault didn't stop there. She was hit across the face seven or eight times, accompanied by shouts from the first German. 'Tell us the truth! Who are you? Who are you working for? You will tell us or face the consequences!'

Sandra was beyond screaming in quite a short while, probably after the fifth or sixth slap across the face.

Bugger you Nazi bastards, she thought. She was determined to tell them nothing. By now, though, her face was bleeding.

'Tell us who you really are or this will get worse for you!' the German shouted at her as the slaps across the face continued.

Sandra became more and more determined the more she was hit. She would never tell them anything. She would die before giving anyone or anything away.

The slapping stopped after a while and the Gestapo officer sitting in front of her said, 'Very well. If you will not talk, we will see what else we can do to persuade you otherwise.'

At this point she could feel her shoes being removed. What are they going to do? she thought. Tickle my feet, perhaps? That would be nice.

'I will ask you once more. What is your real name? Who are you working for? Who are your contacts? Tell us now and you will save yourself a lot of pain.'

Sandra made no response.

'Carry on,' said the Gestapo officer. This was obviously an order.

Sandra felt her left leg being held in a vice-like grip. What are they doing? she thought. It would soon become very obvious.

The German holding Sandra's leg preferred to look away from what was about to happen. He had seen it done before and it was not something anyone would choose to watch. Besides, he thought, the screams of the victim would be more than enough to convey the agony she would be experiencing. He braced himself and held Sandra's leg tightly.

The other Gestapo man was sitting on the floor with a pair of pliers in his hand. He reached out to Sandra's foot and clasped the pliers' jaws on to the nail of her little toe. Sandra let out a scream.

'Your last chance. Tell us now!' the Gestapo officer screamed at her.

Sandra said nothing.

Following the silence, the officer nodded towards the one with the pliers, who tightened his grip on the handles and proceeded to twist and turn them, slowly pulling the nail on Sandra's little toe from its home. Suddenly, the nail was removed, followed by a trickle of blood that splashed on to the floor.

The pain was excruciating. Sandra could not hold back

her cries of agony. This was obviously something she had never experienced before and her SOE training had not prepared her for it. She was near collapse.

'Tell us now or more will follow!' The voice of the Gestapo officer screaming at her made her all the more determined.

'I am innocent! I am innocent,' she cried. 'Please let me go! I have done nothing. Please stop.'

Her cries were loud. They helped mask the excruciating pain in her foot, though not for long.

The Gestapo man slapped her across the face. Sandra was bleeding from her foot and her mouth. She was in agony. Dear God, she thought. How can I survive this? How?

The pliers were again applied to Sandra's toe, the one next to her little toe. She felt the squeeze on her nail, accompanied by the shout 'Tell us now or else!' from the Gestapo officer.

Her silence was, once again, followed by the tight grip on her leg and the appalling pain of having another toenail removed. She felt ready to die. The pain was just too much to bear and mercifully Sandra passed out.

Seeing her become unconscious, the Gestapo men stopped the torture. The officer gave orders for the torturers to leave the room, while he completed some paperwork on his desk. Sandra did not move and, after a while, the blood stopped flowing from her foot and her mouth, though she remained unconscious.

The Gestapo officer finished his paperwork, got up and left the room. Sandra was left alone. After around thirty minutes, she began to come round. The first thing that hit her between the eyes was the excruciating pain from her toes. There was nothing she could do about it, strapped in the chair with her hands tied behind her back, though her legs had been untied by the agents to access her toes. All she could do was try to cope. She had to attempt to escape, impossible as that seemed. The only alternative was more torture, pain and death. She was not ready to die. How could she escape?

Sandra could only guess she was being left alone because it was now night-time. She hoped, but couldn't be certain, that this would give her a few hours of respite. She must try to get out somehow. She looked about the bare room, which contained just the desk and chair, as well as the chair to which she was tied. No windows, one door and one light hanging from the middle of the ceiling. It was still switched on. That's a mistake, she thought. They should have switched the light off. The officer must have forgotten to do it. Good.

Sandra half-stood up and slowly, painfully, moved towards the desk. She could do this as her legs were no longer tied to the chair. She managed to manoeuvre herself and the chair to the side of the desk, where she could see there was a drawer. Might be worth opening, she thought. But how? Well, there was really only one way: by using her teeth to grip the drawer handle and pull it open. Fortunately, none of her teeth had been knocked out during the beatings she had received from her tormentors. She slowly manipulated the chair and herself so that she was bent double by the desk drawer, where she could just manage to wrap her teeth around the handle and gently pull it open. She managed to pull the drawer open about twelve inches before she fell back on the chair, only just managing to stay upright. Now, let's have a look to see if there is anything that can help me, she thought.

The drawer was full of what one might expect: pens, ink

bottles, paper files, a letter opener in the form of a knife and – under a few bits of paper that partially masked its existence – a pistol. Sandra's heart was racing. Got to get that knife out, she thought. Again, her teeth were very useful and, after a few minutes of nearly impossible contortions, she managed to get the knife out and on to the desk top. She grasped it with the ends of her fingers, which were not constricted by the ropes around her wrists. After several attempts, she found she could grip the knife and move it slowly up against the ropes that bound her. This is going to be a long job, she thought.

Slowly and painfully, as the movement of her fingers to get the knife to cut the rope caused some distress through chafing, Sandra succeeded. It must have taken at least two hours, she thought, but there was no way of knowing the exact time. At last, her hands were free of constraint and she quickly managed to release herself from the chair. She stood up. It was painful. Though not as painful as landing in France with a faulty parachute, she thought, looking on the bright side.

What was she to do now? She rummaged in the desk drawer and got out the pistol. She checked it and *yes!* There were bullets in the chamber. Here was a chance to escape and she would make the most of it. Her foot was a mass of blood and pain, but her determination to escape triumphed over all.

Pistol in hand, Sandra hobbled towards the door. She tried the handle. It moved and the door opened. Slowly, she peered out into a rather dark corridor. There was no one around. Right, thought Sandra, I will have to make my way to the outside world and shoot whoever gets in my way. She entered the corridor and turned to shut the door. The door keys were still in the lock and, as she closed the door, she turned and removed them from the lock, placing them in the inside pocket of her blouse. That'll slow them up when they come back, she thought. Sandra made her way along the corridor slowly and painfully, uncertain of exactly where she was going. There were no lights on anywhere, but in the distance she could make out the dim shape of a door. She approached it cautiously and listened with her ear pressed against it. There was no discernible noise from the other side.

'Here goes,' she said to herself as she gently turned the handle and slowly opened the door.

Sandra was hit by the outside air. It was dark. There was no moon. She thought it must be the middle of the night. Some distance away, about fifty yards from where she was standing, was a large building, which she guessed must be the local Gestapo headquarters. There were just two lights coming from it, one at the front entrance and the other from an upstairs window. The rest was in darkness. She had been imprisoned in an outhouse, which she assumed must be where the Gestapo took their prisoners for interrogation. This is not going to be easy, she thought. There must be some guards around and she could only hobble along. But she had to escape.

Gently, Sandra shut the door behind her and slowly moved away from the outhouse and the lights in the building. First, the gravel on the surface near the door hurt her naked, bloody foot, but after a few steps she got on to some grass that stretched towards an outer wall. The wet, cold grass on her foot was soothing for a time. Reaching a wall, Sandra stopped and looked about. The building still displayed just two lights and the rest of the area was in comparative darkness. There was no sign of any soldiers. All she had to do was get over this wall. Could escape be that easy?

Climbing the wall with her damaged foot was out of the question, so Sandra began inching her way slowly around its perimeter, hoping to find a gate through which she could escape. After hobbling along for some distance, she thought she must be on the opposite side of the headquarters from where she started – and then she saw it: a gated entrance. There it was! All she had to do was get through it and be on her way. There was only one problem. There guarding the gate, armed and in uniform, was a German sentry. How was she going to get past him?

Sandra resigned herself to a course of action that would either bring freedom or cause her to face more torture and probably death. She slowly approached the sentry from his blind side and, getting very close to him, raised her pistol and pointed it directly at his head. Now or never, she thought. Suddenly, the sentry turned towards her and began raising his rifle. Some noise she made must have disturbed him. Sandra pulled the trigger and shot the sentry in the face. He fell to the ground.

She didn't wait around. The noise from her pistol would surely have attracted attention from the headquarters. She had to get away as fast as her hobbling would allow. Then she spotted it just by the sentry post: a bike! It must have belonged to the sentry, she thought. No time to waste. Let's go! Quickly, she got on the bike and, ignoring the pain from her foot, pedalled like fury on to the road and away from the headquarters. Behind her, she was aware of some noise that became harder to hear as her breathing became more and more laboured. 'Got to get away, got to get away,' she said to herself. Sandra began to recognise some of the buildings she was cycling past. She knew where to go if she was to stay safe.

Reaching a crossing, she turned right and pedalled furiously for about a quarter of a mile. There was a house at the end of this road where she knew she would be safe. She reached it, got off the bike and began banging at the front door. A light came on within, and the sound of keys turning and bolts being drawn back reached her ears. In the distance, she could hear that the alarm had been raised at the Gestapo headquarters and she guessed soldiers were searching the streets. The door to the house opened and there in front of Sandra, dressed in a rather drab set of pyjamas, stood Michel.

'What?! *Mon Dieu*!!' he exclaimed.

'Let me in. Take the bike! Put out the lights quickly! The Gestapo will be searching the streets now. Move!'

Michel at once pulled Sandra and the bike inside and turned off the lights. They both hurried to the back of the house. Michel closed all the doors behind them and, once they were safely in the kitchen, Sandra sat down and thanked him, just for being there. Michel took the bike into the back garden.

'I'll hide this where no one can find it,' he assured her. Michel took the bike to a group of bushes in the corner of the garden and, pushing some of the branches aside, exposed a small clearing within where he threw the bike, making sure none of it could be seen from outside. He returned to the kitchen to find Sandra slumped in a chair with her head in her hands and trembling. He couldn't help but notice her bloody foot.

'What has happened? Did the Gestapo capture you? What's wrong with your foot?'

'Yes, they caught me. A damned stupid fool I was to fall for such a ruse. Someone spoke to me in English at the train station and I responded. What a stupid thing to do. I am an idiot.'

'No, you are not. You are a brave woman. Tell me what they did to you.'

Sandra proceeded to tell Michel all that had happened since she was captured by the Gestapo. Michel listened and was shocked by the tale. Later, he fetched some warm water and began cleaning Sandra's foot, which was very dirty. She winced as he bathed her toes. Her foot was not a pretty sight. The pain was alleviated slightly by the fact Michel had a bottle of Calvados and filled a glass for Sandra to enjoy while he treated her foot. Michel thought Sandra was marvellous. He already had a very high opinion of her bravery and resourcefulness before she was captured by the Gestapo, and this latest episode made him realise he knew no one who could possibly hold a candle to her courage and ability. She had escaped, single-handed, from the clutches of the Gestapo. She was incredible.

'My glass is empty, Michel.' Sandra was peering at him with a slight smile and a twinkle in her eyes. He quickly stopped bandaging her foot and fetched the bottle of Calvados.

As he refilled her glass, he said, 'Sandra, you must rest. You are safe here and your foot must get better before you can decide what to do next.'

'I have already decided what to do, so don't worry about that.'

'What is it?' Michel was not in the least surprised that Sandra was so far ahead of the game.

'This foot is going to put me out of any serious action for a time. I think the best thing would be for me to return to London and update them on the situation here first-hand. While I'm there, I can get my foot seen to by a doctor, recuperate and then, when it is healed, I will return. I won't be able to visit any doctor or hospital here – it would be too dangerous. Therefore, I am going to need your help in getting back to London. What do you think would be the best method to use?'

'Lysander would be best. I will contact London by wireless tonight and arrange for you to be picked up very soon. Do you agree?'

'Of course.'

Michel continued to attend to Sandra's foot while she enjoyed the sweet brandy of Normandy. It certainly helped to take her mind off the pain.

That night Sandra slept in the attic at Michel's house. She could occasionally hear the sound of cars and footsteps in the street. That would most likely be the Gestapo looking for her. She prayed they would have a fruitless evening.

The next morning Michel left the house with his wireless set to send a message about Sandra to London. He was going to cycle to a remote place somewhere in the nearby woods. He guessed the Gestapo would be on high alert following the escape and would be concentrating on picking up any messages being sent in the area. He could travel quite easily with his wireless. It was the very latest to be dropped into France from London, known as a Type A, Mark III, and came in its own suitcase. Its weight was only nine pounds and Michel could carry it easily while cycling. Even better, this wireless would operate from its own batteries, so it did not need power from an electrical mains supply. This was a very good modification from previous wireless sets because often the Gestapo, while listening in to a message, would cut off the power to a building to see if the message-sending stopped. This would tell them where the message was being sent from and prompt a search of the building and, often, the capture of an agent.

Michel had left Sandra in the house alone. She was fast asleep when he left, which was a good sign considering all she had endured recently. He soon found a suitable spot, where he set up the wireless and quickly sent a message not only requesting Sandra to be picked up, but also asking for more guns, ammunition and explosives to be brought over on the same trip. Michel then cycled back to the house.

Sandra woke up and was immediately conscious of the throbbing pain from her foot. She got out of bed, splashed some water on her face and had a quick wash all over. She would have loved to have a bath, but in the circumstances that was not possible. Once dressed, she went downstairs to the kitchen, where she made some coffee. There was no sign of Michel.

Suddenly, the back door to the kitchen opened and in he walked.

'Good morning, and where have you been?' asked Sandra.

'Out arranging things for this evening. I'm expecting a response sometime around lunchtime today. I hope London can provide all we need. But you look much better. Did you get a good sleep?'

'Oh, yes. Much better than my previous night! Thank you for taking care of me. You are kind. Can I make some porridge for you? I notice there are no eggs or bacon in your cupboard.'

Michel laughed and said, 'Well, it's not good practice to keep luxuries like eggs and bacon in places where they can be easily found. Just a minute.'

Michel went to the corner of the kitchen and moved

a cupboard away from its position next to the wall. Behind it was a little case, from which he produced the luxury items they had just been discussing. Sandra squealed in delight.

'My, you are so clever!' she said, slightly mockingly. 'Would you like me to cook them?'

'Yes, please,' said Michel.

Later, they sat at the kitchen table and shared a feast of two fried eggs and two bacon rashers each. Sandra had also fried some tomatoes that were grown in Michel's garden.

'If only you had some Calvados to go with this,' said Sandra.

They both laughed.

After their sumptuous breakfast, Michel persuaded Sandra to sit still while he once again bathed her foot in warm water and replaced the bandages around her damaged toes. Afterwards, Sandra borrowed a small knapsack from Michel and put what she could into it to help her get home to England. Meanwhile, Michel left the house with his wireless set and proceeded to a safe location to receive the instructions from London.

When he returned he told Sandra, 'You will be picked up tonight at a location some two miles from the barn. The Lysander should arrive around eleven. It will not be easy because there is no moon tonight, but we should be all right if we make sure the landing site is well marked. I know it's early, but I suggest we leave now to get there and put out our markers in good time.'

Sandra agreed, though she knew the other reason Michel suggested leaving now was because it would take her a long time to hobble her way through the forest to the appointed site.

'Come on, then, let's go,' she replied.

Together they left Michel's house and made their way slowly

through the few streets that separated them from the comparative safety of the woods. Once there, Sandra stopped to draw breath and rest her foot, which was now quite painful. Michel helped her where he could, but their progress was slow. They hoped, at least, that there would not be any Gestapo agents on the route they were taking. On several occasions, Sandra had to stop to ease her foot, but eventually and, in good time, they made it to the edge of the landing site, where they sat and rested before laying out the markers. They would light them when they heard the drone of the Lysander.

'I'm going to miss you, Sandra. You have made such a difference to our operations here. I hope your foot soon heals and you can return to help other parts of the Resistance in France. We need people like you.'

Michel's kind comments came completely out of the blue and took Sandra by surprise.

'Oh, I'm just doing my job, but you have been wonderful in helping me. What would I have done without you?'

Michel chuckled and said, 'You would have probably killed more Nazis!'

They both laughed.

'What's that?' asked Michel.

Yes, it was unmistakable – the drone of the Lysander was above them. Michel ran into the field and began lighting the markers. Sandra hobbled towards the nearest ones and lit them. They were all alight by the time the noise of the Lysander became louder and the plane came in to land. They watched as the pilot brought the plane down very neatly and immediately did a U-turn in preparation for take-off. Michel supported Sandra as she staggered towards the ladder at the side of the plane and helped her navigate herself into the cockpit behind the pilot, who was waving at them.

'Strap yourself in,' Michel instructed, and eventually Sandra attached the seat belt around her waist. She turned her face up towards Michel as he responded downwards and they exchanged kisses – rather affectionate kisses.

'Godspeed,' said Michel.

'Adieu, mon special ami.'

Michel clambered down the ladder after helping Sandra secure the cockpit cover.

As he reached the ground, he turned towards the pilot and waved him off. Michel then ran towards the woods. The sound of the Lysander became louder as it began to accelerate and then took off. Michel turned towards the plane when he reached the edge of the wood. It was airborne in a few more seconds and he waved after it.

Would he ever see Sandra again? Would he ever meet anyone as brave and resourceful as her? He had to admit to himself that he was feeling very affectionate towards her. If only circumstances were different! These thoughts raced through his mind as he watched the Lysander disappear into the night. Sandra was on her way back to England.

James Silverstone gave thanks as he banked to port to direct their flight towards England. He thought back to the last time he was here when, but for the villagers who pulled his plane out of the mud, things would have been so different. He would be forever grateful to them.

The flight home would take around two hours and he was eager to get Sandra back to safety. It had only been six weeks since he had seen her plunge to what he thought was her death, and so much had happened in that time. It was now almost three weeks after D-Day and everyone was wondering just how much longer the war would continue. 'Not too much longer,' he hoped. The plane was rapidly approaching the coast of France – once there, at least he would not have to worry about anti-aircraft fire shooting them down.

Unfortunately, he thought too soon. There was suddenly a burst of fire from below and tracers of bullets surrounded the plane. They were close to Le Havre port, which was heavily defended. He should have gone a different route to avoid it, he thought to himself.

Sandra was a little concerned as she was sitting in the rear cockpit. Please don't let us be shot down now, she thought, as the bullets screamed around her.

James took the Lysander even lower towards the ground in an attempt to avoid further gunfire. All seemed to be well for a few seconds, but then the control levers in James' hands developed a mind of their own as the plane was hit by gunfire. He momentarily lost control and the plane seemed to be weaving an up and down path in the sky. Sandra just shut her eyes and prayed.

Only one thing for it now, thought James. He would have to land the plane to try to save them both. The engine must have been damaged by gunfire, because it was now coughing and spluttering as though it had a very bad cold. James quickly surveyed the ground below. They were well outside the town and the gunfire had ceased. He would have to land in a field. He could see a number of areas that might be able to accommodate the Lysander. They were now over farmland. The engine stopped. James fought the controls to bring the plane down. It slowly responded, too slowly. They passed over the field he had aimed for as the plane glided forward. Right, it'll have to be the next one! thought James.

The Lysander skipped over a boundary hedge and James managed to force the controls far enough forward to bring the plane on to the ground in the field. He succeeded in keeping the wings stable and the plane came to a stop just a few dozen yards before the next boundary hedge. James unbuckled his seat belt and threw back his cockpit canopy. Sandra opened her eyes.

James turned to her and said, 'Quick – let's get as far away as we can. The Germans will know they have shot us down and will be here soon. Follow me!'

With that, James leapt from his seat and clambered down the ladder. Sandra followed him, making sure she brought her knapsack with her. Together they ran from the plane towards the edge of the field, where they scrambled through the hedge and into another field.

'Can we stop a minute?' asked Sandra as she looked around. She was glad to rest her injured foot, which was hurting from the running they had done. 'There are some lights over there. That may be the town,' she said. 'Let's head towards them and see what's there.'

'OK,' agreed James.

They headed towards the lights in the distance. This meant negotiating a few more hedges before they were close enough to see just a few houses with their lights on.

'Look! There's the sea. We must be very close to the harbour.'

Sandra motioned to James to stop as she spoke. 'We have to take stock now,' she continued. 'Unless we decide something pretty soon, we will get caught and who knows what then?'

'Yes. Agreed. I certainly do not want to spend any more time as a POW. What do you suggest?' said James.

Sandra was very aware of the pain in her foot. She certainly did not want any more of her toenails removed. 'I think we should steal a boat and cross the Channel. Look, over there in that corner of the harbour. There are plenty of boats. England is only about 100 miles away. I'm sure we'd manage. Let's go for it.'

All this sounded a bit mad to James. He had spent hardly any time at sea, but he was game for anything that sounded possible. They would struggle to link up with the Resistance in Le Havre without any forewarnings of their arrival, and they could not just wait for daybreak and wander around hoping to meet up with some Maquis. They would be spotted by the Gestapo for sure.

'OK. Let's do it,' he said.

They walked down towards the harbour, although how they were going to get a boat and sail across the Channel neither knew. Sandra was glad she had the pistol.

It was now past midnight, and there were very few people around in the streets adjacent to the harbour. It was going to be difficult to find a boat they could use at this time. As they approached the quayside, the sound of festivities got louder and they noticed a café from where the noise was emanating. It was right by the quayside and there were people standing outside, chatting, drinking and enjoying themselves.

'Let's try this out,' said Sandra, 'but let me do the talking. You just play dumb, OK?'

'OK. But I can speak a little French.'

'I think it may be best if you don't, at least for a while until we know who is there.'

As they approached the café, some of the people outside looked towards them and one of them, a young woman, greeted them with, *'Bonjour, es-tu venu loin?'* ('Hello, have you come far?')

Sandra replied, *'Non, nous venons de quitter la maison de mes amis et avons pensé que nous pourrions nous amuser ici.'* ('No, we have just left my friends' house and thought we might join in the fun here.')

Sandra and the young Frenchwoman continued in conversation while James felt a little sheepish and stayed as quiet as possible. He spent his time watching the ten or so people outside the café. It looked very busy inside. They are all having a good time, he thought. It was obviously some kind of a celebration. He wondered what it could be.

After a few minutes, Sandra turned to James and whispered in his ear, 'I think we're all right here. It's a birthday party for that gentleman standing just inside the front door, wearing a hat. All these people here are his friends, and, good news, most of the men here are fishermen. If we can gain someone's trust, we may be able to get one of them to get us across the Channel.'

But how? thought James. To do that would mean having to expose ourselves as Allied agents. Who can we trust? And if we tell someone the facts, will they believe us? They may well think we are German agents trying to catch Resistance members. They might even shoot us!

He returned a whisper into Sandra's ear. 'That is not going to be easy. We must be very careful,' was all he could say.

Sandra nodded and returned to her conversation with the young woman, who was now looking at James, fluttering her eyelashes, and suddenly directed a question at him.

'*Quel est votre nom?*' ('What is your name?')

'James. *Et le vôtre?*' ('And yours?')

'Brigitte.'

Sandra interrupted by telling Brigitte that James was suffering from a throat infection that meant he could not speak properly. Brigitte expressed some concern and asked if she could buy them some drinks. They both accepted with thanks.

Brigitte went into the café to get their drinks. Sandra waited until she was gone and again whispered to James, 'We may be on to something with Brigitte. Her family are fishermen – her two brothers and her father. If we are both sure about trusting her, I could tell her exactly what has happened to us and ask if we could hitch a lift. What do you think?'

James voiced his concerns, but he concluded, 'Let's do it. We are in a desperate situation, so let's just do it and hope for the best.'

'OK,' said Sandra as Brigitte returned with the drinks.

Sandra wasted no time. She took Brigitte to one side and told her of their situation. The reaction was one of surprise. Brigitte then went back inside the café and returned moments later with her father, who was looking very serious. He approached Sandra and, after they exchanged a few words in French, they walked away from the café with James following behind. They stopped a few yards along the road out of earshot of anyone in the café.

Brigitte's father turned towards them and in halting English said, 'I have a boat that could get you across the Channel. I will risk it if you will. It will take about seven or eight hours depending upon the weather. Are you prepared for it?'

'Yes, yes!' was the enthusiastic response from both of them.

'We won't be able to thank you enough,' said James.

'Helping you escape will be enough for me. My brother was shot dead by the Gestapo last year. He had only just returned from a fishing trip and the Gestapo thought he was a smuggler or something. After they interviewed him, they shot him. I hate every one of them. Follow me.'

Hardly believing their luck in finding help so easily, Sandra and James followed Brigitte's father, who they discovered was called Victor, to the quayside. There they boarded a fishing vessel called *L'Homme Tranquille*. Victor had summoned one of his sons, Paul, from the café to help with casting off and the other tasks necessary to get them going.

Sandra and James sat in the cramped wheelhouse, while Victor and Paul steered the *L'Homme Tranquille* towards England. They watched as the lights from Le Havre slowly disappeared into the distance. The only problems they now faced were the weather and any passing German patrol boats.

Sandra looked at Victor and said, 'Which route will you take to get to England?'

'We will sail direct towards Brighton. That's about 200 kilometres. In good weather, it should take us about eight hours, which will mean arriving in daylight at about 9am. We will have to be very careful to avoid English patrol boats, as well as German patrol boats, and your coastal defences, too. They might think we're trying to invade! We may have to show a white flag in order to remain in one piece!'

'Riiiight,' was the slow response from Sandra.

Chapter 10

Neither James nor Sandra managed to sleep during the crossing. They were so thankful at being on a boat with a chance to escape when they could so easily have crashed in the Lysander and both been killed. They continued chatting to each other all the way across the Channel. Paul would occasionally check on them to ensure they were OK. He even made them coffee, though there were no biscuits or food on board. It had been too sudden a departure from Le Havre to make sure they were stocked with provisions. Victor spent the whole journey in the wheelhouse, mostly accompanied by Paul. Sandra promised herself that as soon as she got to London she would contact her mum and dad. Oh, the relief at having survived!

Thankfully, most of the journey was uneventful. The weather

stayed calm and Victor did indeed put up a white flag as they approached the coast of England. There was no interference from any patrol vessels until they were about a mile from land, when a Royal Navy motor torpedo boat approached them at high speed. As it pulled up alongside them, a uniformed Royal Navy officer told them to stop and prepare for boarding. They could see the men on board were all armed and expected trouble. Sandra and James climbed on to the deck of *L'Homme Tranquille* and waited, ready to welcome the boarding party.

Three armed Navy men clambered aboard and demanded they raise their arms, which of course they did. James was the first to speak.

'Welcome aboard, gentlemen. I can't tell you how glad we are to see you. The last few hours have been a bit of a trial for us, but thanks to Victor and Paul we have arrived safely. Please can I speak to your commanding officer?'

James' calm manner and English accent took the three Navy chaps by surprise. They had not expected it. James took advantage of their surprise and continued speaking.

'Let me introduce us all. I'm Flight Lieutenant James Silverstone RAF, and this young lady is Sandra Eden SOE, and these two Frenchmen are Victor and Paul, who have gallantly helped us to escape from occupied France.'

One of the Navy men had already signalled to his captain to come over. As James finished speaking, another Naval officer – a commander – appeared and immediately started firing questions at them.

'Why were you in France? And how did you manage to get a boat and sail across without being blown out of the water by the Germans?'

'We are very fortunate to have met Victor, who is a fisherman, and he agreed to help us get across the Channel. We are in his debt.'

Sandra, who had been silent until now, looked at the commander and said, 'I can't tell you why I was in France or what I did there, because if I did I would have to shoot you!'

There was a momentary silence from everyone, which was broken by the muffled laughter of the three Navy men standing behind their leader, who despite himself managed a smile at Sandra's remark.

'OK. Stay here while I radio base to confirm your identity.'

The commander returned to the ship, leaving them under the watchful eye of the three Navy men. He was gone for about thirty minutes.

Upon returning, the commander said, 'Right-o men, put down your guns. Eden and Silverstone will come with us. The two Frenchmen are free to return to their home, with our fullest thanks for a job well done.'

At this point, the commander signalled to two of his men, who brought some boxes of supplies for the Frenchmen who received them with much thanks. The commander then straightened himself and saluted Victor and Paul, then shook hands with each of them. Sandra and James also thanked Victor and Paul, then made their farewells before boarding the Naval vessel. As *L'Homme Tranquille* turned towards France, Sandra and James waved and waved until the boat was just a small dot on the horizon.

'I pray they get home safely,' murmured Sandra.

By the time they reached the quayside in Brighton harbour it was almost 11am. Sandra and James were collected from there by car and taken to a house on the outskirts of town. It was there that they were debriefed by two army officers and were able to tell of their incredible escape from France.

By now, Sandra's foot was in a bit of a mess. She could feel the wetness of what she took to be blood coming from her toes. She asked for a doctor, after explaining to the two officers why she needed one. They were a little taken aback after listening to Sandra's description of her torture by the Gestapo. A doctor soon arrived and proceeded to bathe and dress her foot.

'You really must keep this wound as clean as possible,' he advised her. 'It may take a year or more before your toenails grow back, but please be careful. They will be very tender for a few weeks.'

'Thank you, Doctor,' said Sandra. 'I promise I will be very careful to try to avoid the Gestapo in future.'

'Quite!' was his terse response.

Once the doctor had finished attending to Sandra's toes, he left the room. Sandra and James were by now very hungry.

'Any chance of some breakfast?' asked James.

'Of course. Follow me,' said one of the officers.

He led them to a small room in the house where a couple of tables were laid out for meals and then called for service from a waitress, who produced two breakfasts and a large pot of tea for them.

'Not quite as good as what I was getting in Normandy!' said Sandra, looking at the single fried egg and two pieces of toast on her plate.

'I bet,' said James.

After their comparatively meagre meal, they returned to the

interview room where they had been debriefed. Only one officer was there now, a Major Lister, who proceeded to tell them what would happen next.

'Sandra, you are wanted back in London. We have arranged for you to catch the train from Brighton to London Bridge tomorrow morning. From there, you are to go to St Ermin's Hotel, where you will be met by the chap in charge – they have not given me his name. From there, anything could happen.'

'Thank you,' said Sandra.

'And James, you are wanted back in Tangmere. We have arranged for you to travel by train to Chichester station, where you will be collected by car and returned to the aerodrome. Any questions?'

'What time will my train be leaving?' asked James.

'Early tomorrow. We have arranged rooms here for you both tonight. You will be taken to the station by car tomorrow. We will also put together a small pack of items to help each of you on your journey. Let me show you to your rooms.'

Major Lister led them both along the corridor towards the small rooms they had been allocated. James was shown his room first. He was exhausted and yearned for sleep. The bed in the room was tempting. He said farewell to Sandra, who embraced him and gave him a huge kiss. She promised that they would get together soon and enjoy themselves over a dinner date. James agreed.

Major Lister then took Sandra further along the corridor to her room, where she was also desperate for sleep. It had been at least two days since she had managed to close her eyes. Oh, the relief of being safe and secure! But she must contact her mum and dad to let them know she was back in England, so she turned to the Major and asked, 'Is there a telephone nearby? I'm concerned that my parents have been told I was missing in action. They probably think I'm a goner. It would be great to phone them and let them know I'm safe.'

'Of course. Follow me,' said the Major.

He led Sandra to an office where there was a phone on the desk.

'Use that one, then you really must get some sleep. I will see you in the morning before you go. Sleep well.'

'Goodnight,' said Sandra. She knew her parents did not have a phone, but their next-door neighbour did. Her plan was to phone them and ask to speak to her parents. She was soon through to the neighbour, who went next door to get Sandra's parents to the phone.

'Is it really you, Sandra?' Her mum was ecstatic. 'Thank God you are alive! We had almost given up hope. Here's your father.'

Sandra spent the next ten minutes talking to her mum and dad, and trying to put them at ease. She told them she would come and visit them as soon as possible, but she didn't know when, as it was impossible at this time. She promised to keep in touch and contact them whenever possible. The parting words between them were long and emotional.

Sandra hung up the phone, dried her eyes, left the office and proceeded to her bed for the night. She was soon fast asleep, with her alarm set for 7am.

The next morning, James and Sandra met over another disappointing breakfast of one fried egg and toast each. The waitress apologised, explaining that bacon and other foodstuffs were not available because they had used all their ration, and they would have to wait a week before they could collect any more.

'Never mind,' said James. 'I'm sure we'll get something more substantial when we get back to base.'

'Yes. Let's hope so,' agreed Sandra.

After finishing their meal, they went for a little walk together, with Sandra limping, around the grounds of the headquarters building. They linked arms during their walk and enjoyed their conversation. They both wondered when they might be able to meet again. It would soon be time to be taken to the train station, where they would have to part.

The car, driven by a uniformed lady from the First Aid Nursing Yeomanry, took them quickly to Brighton station and James was soon on his way to Chichester and then on to Tangmere. Sandra had to wait a little longer for her train to London Bridge. Their parting had been a little emotional for both of them. They parted with a kiss and a hug. Sandra felt very close to James, because they had shared a lot together. James waved to her as his train pulled out of the station. She waved back.

Sandra was soon on the train to London Bridge. She leaned back in her seat and was almost on the point of going to sleep when a passenger sitting opposite said, 'Excuse me, but haven't we met somewhere before?'

Sandra looked at the man who had asked the question. She recalled his face from SOE training, but she was under orders, from that same training, to 'never recognise anyone whom she had met on training if she happened to meet them later.' She was not going to break that order – at least not yet.

'No, I don't think so. What's your name?'

'I'm Simon, Simon Gerrish. But aren't you Sandra? Sandra Eden? We met during training in Scotland last year. Don't you remember? We shared a couple of parachute drops together during our training. You were just so encouraging. What have you been up to?'

Suddenly, the memories of that time came flooding back into Sandra's mind. Yes, she did remember him. They had spent a few days together in Scotland at the SOE training centre in Arisaig House many months ago. She recalled him being something of a devil-may-care individual.

'Well, I can't tell you what I've been doing, or I'd have to shoot you!' Sandra said this with a twinkle in her eye, which went down very well with Simon. 'And, anyway, what have you been up to?'

'I can't tell you that either or I'd have to shoot you, too!' Simon replied.

They both laughed heartily. Though they were under orders not to recognise and talk to each other about their SOE training, they both felt it would do no harm to be sociable, so they were determined to be at least friendly to each other.

Simon said, 'I won't ask you where you are going in London. However, are you free for lunch today? By the time we get to London Bridge, it will be around 12.30pm. We could get a taxi to a very nice place near St James's where they do excellent lunches. Would you like to go?'

'Oh yes, that would be lovely, thank you.' Sandra didn't need much persuading to be treated to lunch – not after what she had been through over the last few weeks! She was determined to have a really good time and she was not due to meet her superior on SOE business until 5pm. Plenty of time to enjoy herself.

The train continued onwards to London Bridge at a steady pace and, as with all trains carrying passengers at that time, it was very crowded. Sandra and Simon were soon surrounded by standing passengers as more and more people got on at the various stations. The last leg of their journey was not the most comfortable. People, many in uniform, were crammed tightly everywhere in the carriage and it was not unusual to have someone's backside a few inches from their faces.

When the train reached London Bridge station, there was a mad dash for the exits. Indeed, some people jumped off the train on to the platform while the train was still moving. Not the safest thing to do, but such was the sense of urgency everywhere that it was a common sight.

Sandra and Simon made their way towards a taxi rank, where they actually managed to find one waiting. As they got into it, Simon said, 'Stafford Hotel, St James's, please, driver.'

'Certainly, sir,' the driver replied, and off they went towards the Stafford Hotel.

Sandra was enjoying herself. She felt at ease with Simon, and the fact that they shared something as secret as being members of the SOE drew them closer together. And being in a taxi! What luxury!

The taxi drew up outside the main entrance, where they both got out, laughing and looking forward to a nice lunch. Simon paid the driver and into the hotel they went.

My, thought Sandra, this is a very grand place.

They were shown to a table in the restaurant by the waiter. Simon seems very much at ease in this atmosphere, thought Sandra. He must be used to this. Perhaps his family are moneyed people.

The waiter gave them each a menu and said, 'What would sir and madam like to drink?'

Simon looked across at Sandra. 'Would you like some rosé wine?'

'Oh yes, please, I do like rosé. But just a small bottle to begin with.' Sandra's eyes were sparkling as usual.

'Small bottle?' The waiter looked concerned.

Simon smiled at the waiter and said, 'That means not a magnum. She is only joking.'

'Certainly, sir.' The waiter turned and left them at the table, pondering where anyone could get such a strange sense of humour. He soon returned with the rosé, which they agreed was an excellent wine, although Sandra couldn't help comparing it with some of the wine she had recently enjoyed on the other side of the Channel. Not bad, though, she thought.

After they had enjoyed the starter course, Simon asked, 'Is Sandra Eden your full name?'

'No. I have a middle name.'

'What is it?'

'Olivia. Olivia after my dear mother.'

Simon muttered 'Sandra Olivia Eden' to himself, then beamed a smile and said, 'You are joking, aren't you?'

'Why on earth would I joke about my name? It is what it is. When I was christened, Mum and Dad weren't to know what the future held for me!'

'True, of course. Still, quite a coincidence, don't you think?'

'Yes, I do.' Sandra did not want to continue with this conversation in what she thought was a pretty pointless manner, so she changed the subject sharply and said, 'And since I'm sure you were about to ask, I'll have a sidecar.'

Simon looked puzzled.

'Surely you've heard of them?'

'Well, yes. It's something attached to a motorcycle, but I imagine you may be referring to something else.'

Sandra rolled her eyes – but not too much because they were also twinkling in their inimitable way – and said, 'It's a cocktail. A cocktail of Calvados cognac and orange liqueur, plus lemon juice.'

'Hmmm, that sounds nice. I think I'll have one, too!'

Together they enjoyed the food and drink on offer in the restaurant. Given Sandra's recent experiences, it was a very luxurious lunchtime indeed. She made the most of it.

'I have to be at St Ermin's Hotel by 4.30pm. I'm due for a briefing there. Where are you going this evening?' Sandra knew it would not be a problem letting Simon know where she was going. His response did not surprise her at all.

'Same place as you. But my meeting is at 6pm, so I had planned to be there by 5.30pm. Shall we share a taxi?'

'Good idea,' said Sandra.

After they had finished their meal together – and had another sidecar each – they collected their coats and made their way to the main entrance, where Simon ordered a taxi.

'Thank you so much for that lovely meal. I hope we get the chance to do it again sometime,' said Sandra.

'My pleasure. I guess we will soon be on other operations. But let's agree to keep in contact and, when the opportunity presents itself, we must get together.'

'Yes, please.'

The taxi took them to St Ermin's Hotel, where Sandra was given instructions to go to the third-floor office of her commanding officer. She bade farewell to Simon. Neither knew when they would be able to meet again, given the nature of their work, but they wished each other good luck and exchanged hugs.

Sandra settled in the chair opposite the desk of her commanding officer, Maurice. He had welcomed her in and congratulated her on her work in France over the last few weeks. She was glad to have it acknowledged.

Maurice, slowly raising his hooded eyes, looked at Sandra and said, 'Your next operation will be in northern France near the city of Amiens, north of Paris. There are a great many things to do there, especially organising the Resistance to help our forces. We have arranged a contact to meet you when you arrive. She is a member of the Maquis. Her code name is Salamander. The plan is that you destroy the main train links between Amiens and Paris, and other rail links between northern France and Belgium. The full plan of operation and all your contacts et cetera will be given to you later this evening at your meeting with our planning team. The idea is that you will be parachuted into France next Tuesday around 11pm, where you will be picked up and transferred to the nearest safe house. Any questions, Sandra?'

'Thank you, Maurice. I look forward to linking up with the French Resistance again, and helping our troops against the Nazi forces in France, but I will not be jumping from a plane wearing a parachute. Thank you.'

Maurice looked surprised. He did not quite comprehend what he had just heard. 'What do you mean? Are you saying you will not go?'

'No. Not that. I want to go and do my bit to defeat the forces of tyranny. It's just that I will not be jumping from a plane using a parachute. You will have to arrange for a Lysander to take me and land in a field, that's all.'

'But that will increase the danger of being caught by the Germans, especially in the area where you will land. There are German forces all around Amiens, and that area is very important in our fight to get through Belgium and Holland and into Germany. Why won't you go by parachute?'

She looked him straight in the eyes and said, very firmly and resolutely, 'Because leaping from a plane with a parachute is too bloody dangerous and I'm too bloody scared!'

SOURCES

Books

Binney, M. 2003. *The Women who Lived for Danger*. Hodder Paperbacks.

Fitzsimmons, P. 2001. *Nancy Wake*. Harper Collins.

Foot, M.R.D. 1984. *SOE: The Special Operations Executive 1940-1946*. Greenwood Press/BBC.

Ottway, S. 2013. *Sisters, Secrets and Sacrifice*. Harper Collins.

Special Operations Executive. 2014. *Special Operations Executive Manual*. William Collins Ltd.

Stilwell, A. 2018. *Secret Operations of World War II*. Amber Books Ltd.

Wake, N. 1985. *The White Mouse*. Pan Macmillan.

Internet

School for Danger: SOE & French Resistance Fight the German Occupation – Restored 1945. https://www.youtube.com/watch?v=YsDTZKbVZiw

Nancy Wake: Gestapo's Most Wanted (French Resistance Documentary) | Timeline. https://www.youtube.com/watch?v=qNXKovYM15A